Sealed

with a Kiss

L. MOONE

CONTENTS

Sealed with a Kiss   1

Author's Note   231

PROLOGUE

* Daniel *

15th July

I almost didn't go.

Actually, I've already missed my chance, probably. After wasting a bunch of time at a train station coffee shop, convinced that I wasn't going through with it, I grew impatient. Did I literally just come all this way just to chicken out? After hiring a dog walker for the day, and everything? If Jack was human, he'd have some choice words for me.

Finally, I get anxious enough to get up from my seat, pay for my coffee, and make my way into the city. The very least I can do is go to the studio, to see if I've really missed out already.

Who knows, they might be flexible enough to give me a second chance? I could make some kind of excuse, justifying my extreme tardiness. Blame it on the train. Or something. Pretend I had my wallet stolen. At least I shouldn't return home a quitter.

The studio looks cold and imposing from the outside. A different world. Inside, magic is made.

Am I seriously still going to try to audition for a dating show, of all things? Apparently, I am. My legs keep on moving one foot in front of the other. I ask reception about the audition, and they send me up some stairs and down a long corridor, until I reach my destination.

My heart is racing and my palms are sweating. This is the dumbest idea I've ever had.

But then, I'm supposed to get out of my comfort zone every so often. Apparently that's good for your personal development.

I don't feel good.

Still, I knock on the door. No answer. I lean in to listen for any noises coming through. That's when I notice just how solid this metal-rimmed door is. It's completely soundproof, no doubt! I can't hear what's happening inside, and they can't hear me knock either.

I push my way through and enter a large, mostly dark hall. There is a partitioned off area nearer to the entrance with some folding chairs, a little table with a bunch of water bottles and sad-looking sandwiches, and not much else. No sign of people.

Maybe they've already gone for the day? I must have blown my chance.

"Hi! Can I help you?" a female voice calls out. I can't quite see where she is, so I walk around to the other side of the partition wall to get a better look.

"Is this the dating show audition?" I ask, still unsure who I'm actually talking to.

When I make it further into the cavernous room, I see them. A couple, sitting at a table, with a camera pointed roughly in my direction. Or rather, the direction of the chair that's set up in front of the backdrop I just walked around.

"Your name, please?" the woman asks.

"Daniel."

She shuffles through her papers, while the two of them exchange a few muffled remarks.

I should really apologize for being late. I should…

The woman waves at me. "You're a little late, but I think we can fit you in. Please take a seat."

I exhale sharply and do as she says. "I almost didn't turn up," I remark, squinting when the light set up near their table switches on and nearly blinds me.

The guy, who so far hadn't spoken to me directly, gets up from his seat and approaches, clip-on microphone in hand. He's frowning. Maybe I interrupted something between the two of them.

I'm not sure how to feel about that. Envy is such a dirty emotion.

"Good to go," the man mumbles, then he nods at me once and takes his seat at the table again. He looks a few years younger than me. Maybe mid-twenties. And tall.

"Why didn't you want to come here?" the woman

asks.

I glance up at her. My eyes have started to adjust to the bright lights. Obviously, she'd ask that. I'm not sure if my honesty would be appreciated right now, but I've got nothing else.

"Would you want to have a blind date on TV?"

The two of them exchange a knowing look. Yeah, they're definitely together, and for a long time too. They look so comfortable in each other's presence. I wish I knew what that feels like. To have someone who understands you so intimately, you don't even need words anymore to express yourself.

"I suppose not," she says.

"It's a lonely world out there. You guys are lucky to have each other, is all I'm saying."

The man nearly jumps out of his seat at my remark. "Oh, we're not a couple!"

Wow. That was defensive! His reaction causes me to immediately apologize for my words.

So much for trying to break the ice and make up for being late.

The woman stares at the man for a moment. They might not be a couple, but there's definitely something going on. And I've struck a nerve in both of them. Me and my big mouth.

"Why don't you tell me why you *do* want to be on the show? After thinking it over," she asks.

Her tone is firmer now. Less friendly than before.

I'm definitely not getting shortlisted now.

"I've come a long way these past five years."

"Right." She impatiently gestures at me to keep talking, so I take a deep breath to prepare myself.

"As you might have gathered from my application, I've had some problems. Anxiety and such." Another deep breath later, I carry on. I hate talking about all of this stuff.

"After spending all of my teens and twenties as a recluse, pretty much, I'm getting to a point in my life where I know I need to make some changes quickly. I've worked hard on myself; physically as well as mentally, so I hope that now I'm ready for the next step."

"How much weight have you lost, exactly?" she asks.

I try not to scoff. People always want to know about *that*. They never care to think about everything else. How much I had to work on my mental space first of all.

"About two hundred pounds."

Both of them lean back in their seats. "Wow."

I have to remind myself that I'm not here to educate people on the importance of mental health and how it affects everything in your life, especially your physical health. I'm here to find love. Or at least companionship. Lecturing people on their inherent biases and misconceptions isn't going to help my case at all.

"I know I haven't quite reached my goal yet," I mumble. "But, shit, I'm approaching thirty-five. If not now, then when? And I haven't had any luck dating on my own, so…"

I hope that at least gets my point across. They're trying to make a dating show. I want to go on a date. All this weight loss stuff is secondary. But hey, if it gets me in the door, am I really going to complain about it? Or worse, sabotage myself by acting pissy?

Luckily, the remaining questions focus less on my backstory and more on my vision for the future. What would my ideal partner be like; am I looking to settle down; that sort of thing.

Finally, we're getting into the real issues.

I explain that I'm eager to have a family. That looks don't matter to me as much as character does. Caring. Honesty. Loyalty. That's probably my number one priority in a potential partner. Someone by my side, who doesn't change their colors as soon as the going gets tough. My past has taught me that you just never know what life has in store for you.

And while I try to be as eloquent yet accurate as possible in my answers, I also keep looking at the two of them while they observe me from their audition desk set-up.

I wonder what the real story between them is. They're definitely close, even if they're not a couple.

Friends with benefits, maybe? But then again, why was *he* being so defensive earlier? Is she the only one with romantic feelings? That doesn't make sense either. She's adorable and he is… well, just a regular guy with a bit too much padding around the middle. A bit like me, maybe, just a few years younger and an inch or so taller.

There's no way in hell I would turn down a girl like her. *No way.*

What's *his* problem?

The pause after my final answer lingers until it starts to feel awkward. Do they expect me to elaborate some more? My speculations about their relationship have made me lose my train of thought, so I keep quiet until finally the woman breaks the silence again.

"I would like to shortlist you. But you should know that there are very few spots available for this first season, so I can't promise anything right now. You'll hear back over the next week or so if you've made it onto the show."

I don't know whether to be happy about that, or terrified. "Thank you so much."

Jesus. This was by far the weirdest thing I've ever done. My therapist would be proud. If I had one of those, and I don't.

"Take care, Dan," she says.

I unclip my microphone with trembling fingers

and place it on the chair, before awkwardly waving goodbye at the two of them. After that, I can't get out of there fast enough.

It's too early to tell if this was the dumbest thing I've ever done, but it's definitely the most bizarre.

CHAPTER ONE

*** Kate ***

15th August

"Kate! Long time, no speak!"

"Yeah! How have you been, girl?" I answer.

Why on earth would Claire call me out of the blue on a Wednesday evening when I want nothing more than to finish my work and get the hell out of here? I haven't heard from her since… I suppose it's been a few months. We were supposed to meet for coffee, but the plan never materialized.

"Funny you should ask. So, I'm shooting this reality show, right?" Claire says.

I barely get a chance to respond as she tells me all about her latest project. Last I heard Claire was doing some kind of cooking show. I guess in her line of work, projects tend to come and go pretty quickly.

Now, apparently, it's blind dates. Totally unscripted, actual real people going on real dates. With a camera crew recording their every move. Those kinds of shows are my guilty pleasure. The more cringey the better.

I wish my work was that exciting. Actually, no. I'd hate to have an unpredictable job with erratic hours. Grace would hate it even more. At least now I have evenings and weekends off to spend with her. She is my world, and makes any job—even an excruciatingly boring one like this—worth having.

"So, what do you think?" Claire asks.

I'm not sure how to reply to that.

"Sounds exciting," I say.

"So, you'll do it?"

Wait, what?! "I wouldn't go that far!" I protest.

Jeez, what have I almost accidentally agreed to?

"But you're always complaining about how hard it is to find a nice guy to settle down with. Someone kind, who really wants to start a family; someone who will listen and actually care. I'm telling you, he's perfect! And plus, you'll get a Michelin star meal all paid for. I can't share the name of the chef whose restaurant we're shooting at until you sign an NDA, but he's a big shot. It'll be worth it just for that, I promise. Plus, I can throw in a world class make-over by our on-set stylist if you'd like…" Claire chatters on.

"I don't need a make-over!" Although… I stretch out my neck and roll my shoulders back and forth. If she adds on a spa day as well, I might let her tempt me into it.

"You'd be doing me a huge favor. If I don't turn

in this last episode, the network is definitely not going to hire me for the next season. This is my one shot, Kate."

I stay quiet. This is a dumb idea. No matter how much I love reality shows, I've never actually wanted to appear on one.

"Daniel is *totally* your type."

I roll my eyes. "I very much doubt that."

"Don't think I never noticed you always went for a particular sort of guy. He's the real deal, I'm telling you."

I scoff. "Like you always went for the jocks with attitude problems in college?"

"Okay. How about I send you his audition video and you make up your own mind, huh? But do *not* share it with anyone, okay? They'll replace me in a heartbeat if they find out I'm even talking to you about this!"

Despite everything, my curiosity is piqued. Ever since I started listening to her again, I managed to piece together most of the situation at hand. She's got a contestant she needs to set up on a date. For whatever reason, that's proving difficult, so she wants *me* to go on her show and act all agreeable so the date looks good on camera. And apparently he's exactly my type, whatever *that* means.

"Fine! Send me his video."

"You're the best!" Claire exclaims.

"I haven't said yes yet!" I try to warn her, but she's already hung up.

Ugh. With friends like these…

"Kate, have you got a moment?" This very specific combination of words, spoken at five past five, never fails to dampen my spirit. I knew I should have ignored Claire's call and finished up for the day instead of lingering at my desk long enough to give anyone a chance to derail my evening plans.

"What's up, Evelyn?" I ask, a fake smile plastered on my face. I really just had to jinx myself today by thinking of this job as having predictable timings, didn't I? Only to have *her* come in and prove me wrong.

"These reports don't look quite right to me. Would you be a dear and go through the figures just to make sure? By tomorrow morning, please. I'll need them during the meeting at nine."

I stare at the fat stack of papers in her hand, then at the wall clock. Every single one of my colleagues has their heads down in intense focus.

"I suppose if I take them home… As you know, I have to go pick up Gracie from day-care soon," I mumble. Why does she always come to me with her last minute crap?

"I knew I could count on you." Evelyn flashes her teeth at me. It looks more like a snarl than a grin. Then she turns around and leaves me just as abruptly as she turned up moments earlier. This is just typical.

My phone buzzes on my desk, and Claire's name flashes across the otherwise darkened screen. Suddenly the prospect of watching her super secret reality dating show audition tape is a lot more exciting than the drudgery Evelyn has dumped in my lap. There's no harm in just taking a look, right? Even if I'm *so* not interested in actually appearing on the thing.

I'd rather check a whole mountain of reports every night after work than actually have a first date on camera with the whole country watching. No matter how supposedly perfect the guy is. Or how very lonely it has been to wake up to a cold side of the bed next to me every morning. Yeah, I'm just going to watch the video, because I promised I would. Maybe fantasize a little about what it would be like to live someone else's life, and then call up Claire to refuse. If she needs someone to go out with some dude who apparently can't smooth-talk his way through a date he literally signed up for himself, she can just hire some aspiring actress like all the other supposed reality shows do.

And I'll be ready to watch said episode with a bucket of popcorn when it airs. But first…

I rush to pack up my stuff, including those hateful reports. So typical that I should be saddled with the tedious task of checking figures when Evelyn will be the one to take credit for all the work in front of upper management in the morning. On days like these it feels like she is the evil stepsister to my Cinderella, except there's no ball to go to, and no prince to marry to drag me out of this drudgery.

Unless… I'm growing more and more curious about Claire's video, but I'm going to have to resist. At least until I pick up Grace and get started on dinner. No matter how much it pains me.

***

With dinner done, the kitchen tidied up, and Grace comfortably curled up on the sofa watching *Frozen* for the thousandth time this month, I finally manage to catch a breath. And that's when I remember the reports Evelyn handed me before I left work. So much for being able to unwind tonight.

"Mom! Mom! My favorite bit is going to start!" Grace calls out.

I can't help but smile as she jumps up from the couch and starts dancing along, even though I've seen this particular performance so many times before already. And if I'm totally honest, I'm quite tired of every single song from the movie by now, especially this one.

Still, she's just too adorable, with her wavy, shoulder length hair flying up in the air while she spins around on her own axis. I vaguely remember being obsessed with *The Little Mermaid* when I was

Gracie's age, so I can't blame her for wanting to watch literally nothing else lately. Of course, I took things a step too far when I insisted I wanted to dye my hair bright red at the ripe age of six. Thankfully Gracie hasn't demanded anything more drastic than the occasional braid, so I haven't had to play the bad guy and refuse. Yet.

Once her dance number is over, I applaud enthusiastically and she does a little bow. This right here is why I haven't left my job yet, no matter what Evelyn keeps throwing into my lap. It's these moments at home with Grace which make life worth living.

I check the time before walking over and putting my arms around her. How big she is already! But not big enough to stay up late on a weekday.

"That was brilliant," I tell her.

She hugs me back and gives me a peck on the cheek. "Can I watch it again? Just that bit?"

"Tempting as it is, you know what time it is, don't you?"

She shrugs. "But I'm not tired yet!"

"I know, but once you change into your jammies, brush your teeth and get into bed, you will be."

"But…"

"You can watch it again tomorrow."

"Promise?"

"Promise."

And that's pretty much how that goes every day as well. I get Gracie and her favorite toy—a bright blue stuffed octopus named Ed—out of the living room and into her room. She doesn't need much prompting to brush her teeth, and before I've even realized what's happened, she's in bed with the covers pulled up to her chin, pretending very hard to fall asleep.

I know she'll be up to play as soon as I close the door behind me. And I guess she knows that I know. But that's okay. She's a good kid otherwise. Not nearly as rebellious as I was in my day.

There's still plenty of time for that, I suppose.

"Love you, sweet pea," I whisper as I caress her blonde hair and give her a little kiss.

Her eyes are squeezed shut a little too tightly. She's definitely pretending.

"Nighty night!" I say while making my way out of her room. I pause for a moment after closing the door, and sure enough, I hear a rustle shortly after.

It's fine. She'll settle down soon enough.

And I have plenty to worry about as it is. Those damn reports aren't going to check themselves. Upon heading back into the open plan living area, I find myself walking straight to the fridge. There, I pull out the half-empty bottle of wine waiting for me, and pour some into the nearest glass I can find. Armed with newfound resolve as well as liquid courage, I settle down on the sofa with Evelyn's reports and get started.

And then my phone buzzes with a text. I want to ignore it and get through this bullshit already. But curiosity and procrastination win out.

Claire: "So… what did you think?"

Oh crap.

Another big sip of wine later, I find myself opening the message with the video. Just five minutes. I can always do the reports after that…

So I tap on it, switch to full screen mode, and find myself holding my breath as my heart rate surges for no good reason at all. There isn't even anyone in the frame yet. Just the interior of a bar, with some wait staff milling around in the background. The place has classy decor and the selection of drinks lined up on the shelves looks impressive. But it's still just a bar like so many others.

The camera pans to the door, and in walks a man who looks to be in his mid-thirties, maybe. I like how he carries himself while he says hello to the waitress greeting him on his way in. There's a certain confidence about him. A certain… *Je ne sais quoi*. Like he knows who he is and isn't interested in pretending otherwise.

I can't quite explain it. But I like it. Claire was right that he's my type. From the robust physique to the warm expression in his eyes. I'm not sure how to feel about that. Am I really that predictable?

He sits down on a bar stool and exchanges a bit of small talk with the bartender. The sound isn't super clear, so I can only understand fragments of the conversation.

After that, the camera pans around again towards the door, and in walks a woman. She's dressed to the nines. Maybe even a bit overdressed. Or maybe it's the hair and make-up that puts me off. In any case, I already dislike her. It occurs to me that her mannerisms vaguely remind me of Evelyn. No wonder I'm suspicious of her from the get go.

The man at the bar, whom I'm assuming to be Daniel, gets up to greet her, and they awkwardly shake hands. Weird way to start a date, but then who am I to judge? I've never had a first date with half a dozen cameras pointed my way.

It's pretty clear right from the beginning that there's no chemistry. None. I blame the woman, because Daniel is delish to me and I don't even know the first thing about him yet.

I'm on edge watching it. My hands have grown clammy. Like I wasn't supposed to see.

Didn't Claire say she was sending me an audition video? This looks more like raw footage from an actual first date. Not what I was expecting at all.

Nope. I don't want to see any more. It's painful, though I'm not sure why exactly. I love cringey reality shows usually. Why should this be different? Maybe it's the awkward editing. It looks like a hidden camera prank, not a dating show.

It's as if I can feel Daniel's awkwardness like it's my own. Again, weird. I don't even know him… Yet?

The conversation doesn't flow, despite his best efforts. He even tries to crack a few jokes, which I'd find hilarious, if only the atmosphere between the two of them wasn't so heavy. Then he keeps looking off to the side, presumably at Claire or someone else from the crew, who might be giving directions or just observing the action. As if he's trying to tell them to stop shooting. That this isn't going to work.

Ugh. I try to shake off the anxiety that's crept over me while watching, but I'm having a hard time with it. Second-hand embarrassment.

When Claire called earlier, my first instinct was that as much as I love these things as a viewer, I would never want to be a participant in something like this. And this video has done nothing to convince me otherwise.

Except…

God, Daniel is really cute though. Like, *super* cute. I love how his brown hair is slightly longer on top. The well-kept beard and denim shirt. He's got a bit of a blue collar vibe to him. And just the right amount of meat on his bones for my liking. Like you could rely on him to hunt for food and gather firewood to keep you warm and fed through the winter.

Of course that's some fantasyland bullshit. But still.

And during the few close-up shots in the video, I nearly felt my heart stop when he looked right at the camera. Such kind eyes. Dreamy and deep. I just know I would melt immediately in his presence.

He's my kind of guy. If only circumstances were different… If I can convince Claire to hire some actress to get his episode done, and then after it airs I could ask to be introduced as a fan… Or something. God, that's even more pathetic isn't it?

Claire has put me into a tight spot! I really want to meet this guy. Shit, that video made me want to drag the other woman out of there by her hair and take her place. If only nobody was watching…

Before I can gather my thoughts, my phone rings. Claire. Of course.

"Hey…" I answer.

"I thought I'd find out what you thought… You haven't gone to bed already, have you?" Claire asks.

I catch myself mindlessly nibbling on my fingernails and force myself to stop. Jesus, it's been ages since I've last done that.

"You've put me into a tough position here," I tell her. "Firstly, are you sure you sent me the right video?"

"I think so. Why?"

"Well, it very much looks like you sent me footage

of an actual date, not an audition video."

Claire inhales sharply but doesn't immediately reply.

"Right. Okay, so that thing I said earlier about not telling anyone about this? That, times a hundred. Please delete that video for me as soon as we get off this call, yeah?"

"Like, who am I going to tell? Don't worry about it."

"Of course. But still."

I pinch the bridge of my nose and close my eyes. This is so stupid. Why am I so nervous about saying no to Claire?

"Look, I appreciate what you're doing here. You want your show to be a success, but…"

"It's not just that."

"I just don't think—" I make a face at the phone. *Come on! Are you going to make me spell this out? Let me off the hook already!*

"This is going to sound stupid, but… I really want this to work out. Not for the show—okay, not *just* for the show. But for Daniel."

"What do you mean? He seems like a perfectly nice guy. Why did he sign up for your show, anyway? What's the catch?"

"That's why I meant to send you the audition tape. Crap. Well, let's just say he's had some issues in the past."

I frown. Issues, like what? Is he a reformed criminal or something? Surely Claire wouldn't try to set me up on a date with someone dodgy? I've got Gracie to think about here as well!

"Do I dare ask? What are you trying to rope me into here exactly?"

"Look, it's like you always said. You want a nice, dependable guy in your life. Someone who wants a family as much as you do. Someone loyal, who will stand by you no matter what, yeah?"

"Yeah…"

"This is your guy. Here I go again spilling secrets, but we've got a licensed therapist on the show, evaluating the contestants and their matches."

"Okay…"

"Daniel is legit. He's been through a lot, with his upbringing and everything, and for whatever reason all the women who wrote in seem to be more interested in having their fifteen minutes of fame rather than actually giving a genuinely good guy a chance."

I roll my eyes. Yeah, because anyone who just wants someone nice to settle down with is not going to want to do it on camera. Like yours truly.

"All I'm saying is he deserves a real shot, okay? And this from someone who didn't want to sign him in the first place. And don't you tell anyone I said that either."

"Why didn't you want him on the show?" I ask, frowning again.

"Because… How do I say this… Because he's not…"

My heart is racing again now. I need to know what she really thinks, but a part of me really doesn't, for fear of it messing up the fantasy.

"You *cannot* tell anyone this. Especially him."

"If you want me to do this, you owe me your honest opinion about the guy. It's not just me and what *I* want in life. It's Grace, too."

"Right. Well, he's just not had much luck in the past, you know? I wasn't sure if he'd come across charming enough on TV. Sure, a bit of awkwardness sells, but we're also trying to create a fantasy here. I want the viewers to wish it was *them* on the date, and Daniel isn't your typical—"

"Your typical *what?*"

"He's a nice guy, but I worried that he's not what most of our viewers would go for."

This observation makes me angry, and not just on his behalf.

"But you thought *I* would."

"I know you would, because once I got to know him I realized he's a real gem. Heart of gold."

"But?"

"Kate, I'm giving away too much already."

"You want me to do this or not?" I blurt out.

Shit. Am I really considering this, depending on her answer? I feel manipulated. Like all the secrecy has been designed to get me invested and actually argue with her *in favor of* doing the show.

"He's…"

"Tell me already!"

"He's a virgin, Kate. I didn't want to shortlist him because he's a thirty-four year old virgin. And not for religious reasons… If you tell anyone, I'll hunt you down."

CHAPTER TWO

*** Daniel ***

I run my hand across my chin like I usually do when I'm nervous. But rather than being able to comb my hands through my thick beard, I'm greeted by prickly short hair. The stylist on set, Nicole, suggested that I clean up the beard after the first disaster date, and I'm still not used to the change.

Apparently, the carefully styled look is more youthful, but I hate it. Long beards are excellent camouflage. For double chins and pudgy jawlines, as well as inconvenient emotions. It's still there, somewhat, but I feel rather exposed and not like myself at all.

And for what? The show hasn't worked out quite how I hoped it would. Despite Owen's assurances that his matchmaking methods are totally scientific and should work on everyone, apparently they don't work for me. Despite sitting together for ages, working through all his questionnaires and having my expectations examined from all angles... Presumably my matches had to undergo the same vetting process. And yet they were nothing like I'd expected.

Sure, both of them were gorgeous, but looks weren't even in the top ten of my priorities. I couldn't shake the feeling that both were disappointed when they saw me. Not knowing what someone looks like in advance is pretty much the point of a blind date, but especially the first one, Janet, was clearly expecting someone else. It was embarrassing, and I'm having a hard time not taking it personally.

If Owen's methods are really that foolproof, what does it say about me that so far things haven't worked out? That's the question I try not to think about the most, because some of the potential answers will send me straight back into a place I don't want to go back to.

While I make it a point to arrive early for today's shoot, a part of me wishes I'd never auditioned for this shit show at all.

Was my life really so bad before all this? Fine, I didn't have the kind of love and companionship I'd been craving, but I had a pretty good thing going with Jack. The two of us against the world.

He might not be able to reply when I talk to him, but that just makes him an excellent listener. And the way he greets me like a long lost friend every time I come home? I mean, who wouldn't want that in their lives? He's kept me on the straight and narrow and helped me climb out of the hole I've been stuck in for years. Plus, I've never had to worry about him rejecting me based on my looks or anything else.

Maybe all this dating nonsense hasn't worked out because deep down I'm not ready for it. It's a big step, letting someone else into your life and into your heart. Maybe I can reframe what happened in a positive way? Have I dodged a bullet I didn't even know existed?

Thank god today's shoot is the last attempt. So I just have to suck it up and survive the next few hours. And try not to let it get to me.

This time, I won't go into it with false hope. We're well past that now. Maybe, if I keep my expectations low enough, I can come out of this ordeal unscathed.

"Hey, Daniel!" Jill greets me as I enter. I nod and force a smile.

It's not her fault this hasn't worked out. It's not even Claire's fault, even if she is the executive producer. I blame Owen for bragging about his process so much that I didn't consider the possibility of failure. Relationship expert, my ass.

I'm still in a mood when Jill ushers me into the make-up area.

"Hey there, Dan." Nicole, the on-set stylist, rests her hand on my shoulder as I sit down.

I can't muster anything beyond a short *hi*.

"How are you feeling about today? I think it'll be third time lucky."

"Mhm."

"For sure, I've just seen your date come in, and I think this is going to work out wonderfully," Jill chimes in.

I eye both of them suspiciously.

"That's what you said the last time," I remark.

Jill shrugs. "Well, okay, but it really is different this time."

"Uh-huh."

"Cheer up, at least you'll get a nice meal out of it. Unlike the rest of us who have to make do with these sad looking sandwiches," Nicole says.

I glance over at the array of food laid out for the crew and keep quiet. It's not in the same league as the three course meal waiting for me, but it looks okay enough. Still, no matter how many Michelin stars this restaurant has, I'd rather take a cold sandwich over being humiliated on camera again for the third time in two weeks.

"Cool, cool. Wanna switch places?" I ask Nicole, who responds with a stifled chuckle, before running her fingers through my hair, applying just a little bit of product in an attempt to tame it.

Hell, I would have had a better time having sandwiches *with* Nicole than the fancy meals I've shared with my previous dates. At least she has a sense of humor. And the stakes wouldn't be so high, because it'd just be friendly.

"So, how are things between you and Damien?" I

ask Jill, who turns a shade darker immediately.

"Great." She clears her throat. "Yep, we're great."

Nicole shoots a knowing glance at me through the mirror.

"She's awfully coy about her own relationship, isn't she? While recording half a dozen strangers being all vulnerable and going on blind dates on camera," I comment.

Nicole snickers, prompting Jill to elbow her.

"Hey, hey! Don't assault my stylist. If today's date magically does work out, it'll be entirely because of her efforts to make me look presentable!" I protest.

"You…" Jill wags her finger at me, but doesn't finish her mock threat.

The crinkle in the corner of her eye betrays that she doesn't really mind me pulling her leg. Good. I might test her limits at times, but that's just because the whole will-they-won't-they situation with Damien has intrigued me right from when I first saw them during the audition. I'd love to know what actually happened between them, simply because of the weirdness I observed that day.

Still, I don't actually want to offend her. The entire crew have been really kind throughout, and it's not their fault that my dates haven't worked out. If it hadn't been for them, I would have been out of here halfway through the first date itself.

"Well, think whatever you want. I'm going to go

check on *your date* now," Jill teases. "And I'd better warn her about how nosy you are about other people's private lives."

Nicole starts coughing into her make-up bag behind me; presumably she's pretending not to laugh some more.

"Good idea, Jill. If she can't handle the real me, then we might as well save everyone some time and pull the plug now."

Jill makes a big show of rolling her eyes at me before walking off. Meanwhile, I sit back in the make-up chair and try to relax, while Nicole puts the bare minimum of powder and whatnot on my face.

"You're relentless, you know that?" she tells me.

I shrug. "Aren't you curious about what's going on with them?"

Nicole grins at me through the mirror. "Oh, I already know quite a bit."

"Do you?"

She leans in a little bit. "Yeah, so obviously don't tell her I told you, but they moved in together."

"Really!"

"Yep. All this while, they were pretending not to be an item at all, and suddenly they decide to move in together within a month of coming out to everyone on the crew. Suspicious, huh?"

"A month! That's like…" I frown while trying to work out what the date today is. "That's when my audition was," I mumble to myself.

Nicole cocks her head to the side and nods slowly.

I can't help but shake my head at myself. The way Damien reacted to my ill-timed remark about them being a couple does suggest that maybe things really did move that quickly. Maybe they really were just friends before, like they told all their colleagues. I wish I knew what changed things around for them. I might learn a little something.

"Well, good for them," I say.

Nicole nods.

"Nicole, your coffee," another female voice interrupts. I spot Jill's assistant, Lily, in the mirror behind the two of us.

"Thanks, darling," Nicole tells her. "How are you holding up, everything alright?"

"Oh, you know… Still alive." Lily forces a smile while handing Nicole her coffee, before rushing out of there without making eye contact with either of us even once.

Nicole glances at me in the mirror before taking a sip. "She's been going through a tough break-up. Poor thing."

"That's sad," I say.

"Mhm." Nicole keeps her eyes trained on me for another second or so. "You don't read the tabloids, do you?" she finally asks.

I shrug and shake my head, while wondering how

that question relates to Lily and her rocky love life. "They're not my cup of tea."

"Figures."

I'm about to ask Nicole what she's hinting at, when Lily rushes back again to tell me it's time for me to go on. Guess I'll never know…

Shit, I don't know why I signed up for this. Willingly volunteering for my own slaughter.

As with the previous two attempts, I enter the restaurant first to wait for my date by the bar. Third time lucky? Unlikely.

This time, rather than fighting the butterflies of anticipation in the pit of my stomach, I'm filled with a sense of certain doom. This is *not* going to work out. I don't know why I ever thought it would.

Today is going to end exactly the same as the last two dates, with one notable difference: I'm seeing it coming already. At least I'm prepared for it. Sort of. And then I'll be free. There will not be another attempt after this.

I go through the motions of walking through the doors towards the bar counter, ignoring the spotlights and the camera lenses and Jill and Claire and the rest of the crew waiting around just beyond the light. The bartender asks me what I would like and I'm about to order the same exact thing as last time—a Diet Coke—when I change my mind. It's my last time here. Everything's on the house. Why the hell not have a Scotch instead, something fancy? Just one can't do any harm.

He's just pouring it for me when I hear the door behind me. The same door I'd walked through seconds earlier.

I don't even know if I want to turn around, but I do, as if on cue. Like one of Pavlov's dogs, I jump to the tune.

A woman enters. She looks flustered, as though she's not sure this is the right place. Her eyes meet mine and I'm dead. Gone.

It's as if my consciousness steps out of my body for the next bit. I observe her walking towards me with renewed confidence. Long strides, longer legs. A little flutter in the corner of her mouth, turning into a radiant smile. Before I can fully gather my thoughts, or my words, she stands in front of me.

"Hi."

You had me at 'hi.'

I stretch out my right hand in her direction, unsure of what else to do, when she leans in and gives me a little side-hug. God, her scent is intoxicating. The fleeting touch of her hand on my side throws me off kilter. Her hair, so silky and soft, simply begs to be touched. I don't, of course, because I'm not a creep.

"Hi," I mumble.

"I'm Kate. What's your name?"

"Daniel."

There she stands for a moment, smiling up at me.

Again. She's gorgeous. Where the hell do they keep finding these beautiful women? To go on a date with *me*, no less. Isn't it obvious that this is never going to work?

Shit, I really want it to, though. I want her to keep smiling like that. Like she really means it.

"Nice. Do you come here often?" she quips.

I can't help but chuckle, even if the answer hurts. But she can't know that. Maybe that's what makes it funnier, in a morbid way.

"Hopefully not anymore," I mumble under my breath.

It was a nice idea, not to get my hopes up. An idea I forgot about the moment she walked in. This one's going to hurt way more deeply than the ones who came before.

CHAPTER THREE

"Do you come here often?" Did I literally just say that? What on earth is wrong with me?

I thought I was prepared, because I already knew what he looked like from the video Claire sent me on Wednesday. But sometime between the pep talk Claire's second-in-command, Jill, just gave me in the dressing room, and me opening the door to the bar I'd seen in the video, something short-circuited in my brain, and I lost like fifty points off my IQ.

Stupid and ill-timed.

Daniel doesn't *look* like he took offense to it. If I can shut my mouth long enough to gather my thoughts, maybe all isn't lost yet. It's hard, though. It's impossible to focus while he has his eyes on me.

Despite what I promised Claire, I never deleted that video off my phone. Instead, I've been watching and re-watching the beginning of it endless times. Just the bit before things get awkward. And I've been imagining myself there instead of the stupid cow who rejected him. Whatever her name is.

What I would do. What I would say…

It started off as a way to remind myself why I went along with this crazy idea in the first place. Not just because I don't know how to say 'no' to people. To meet *him*.

But by now, I've become so hopelessly obsessed, I watched it on the way over just to see his face. And now that he's standing right in front of me, I'm completely unprepared anyway.

"What will you have?" Daniel points at the bar behind him.

I don't know. Jesus. I have no idea!

"I'll have whatever you're having," I finally say.

He smiles and I'm dead. Only when he turns around to talk to the bartender can I breathe a little.

He's different in person. And also exactly the same.

Quite a bit taller than me—which isn't hard to do since I'm only five-four—and positively cuddly-looking. Just my type, like Claire said. And his cologne is going to haunt my dreams from now on, I already know it.

He picks up the amber-colored drink the bartender has just poured and hands it to me. Our eyes meet and I know I'm in danger. In danger of doing something even stupider. Like fall for him within the first five minutes. With all these cameras pointed at us, recording my fumbling for all the world to see.

Jesus Christ, I don't even know where to look

right now, so I just smile up at him.

"Thanks."

"Cheers," he says.

I raise my glass in his direction, then take a sip. Whoa, okay. That's a lot of flavors. I should have just asked for a glass of wine.

"Sorry, I do hope the drink is okay."

"Fine, yeah. I just wasn't expecting the intensity of it. Single malt?" I ask.

"Yeah. I don't drink often, but occasionally I like to treat myself."

I'm about to say me neither, when I remember my growing wine collection at home. I blame it on Evelyn riling me up at work almost every day lately…

"It's important to treat yourself at times," I say instead. Like at the end of a stressful day. When you're the only grown woman you know who still gets homework assigned to them.

"What else do you like to do to unwind?" I add.

He likes to read. And spend time in nature. It all sounds so quaint and nice and miles removed from the guys in my past.

"Sports?" I can't stop staring at him, waiting for our eyes to cross next. I must look psycho, with a dumb smile plastered permanently on my face.

He shakes his head, almost apologetically. "I might just watch the Olympics, whenever they're on. Otherwise, not a fan."

Swoon. A guy who doesn't watch sports. Seems like Claire found me a needle in a haystack.

"How about you?" he asks.

"Oh…" I bite my lip and finally look away. "I don't get a lot of spare time because work takes up such a large part of my day… But curling up on the sofa with a good novel is my idea of a Friday night well spent as well." A lie by omission. Nowadays, the only books I tend to read with any regularity are Gracie's bedtime stories.

We chat a little more at the bar. About this and that. Work. Our shared love for police procedurals on TV. I give up on the Scotch about halfway through the glass and set it aside.

I can't remember the last time I felt this way. This light, fluttery feeling in my chest every time we make eye contact. It's almost too much. And with every passing minute, it just keeps on getting stronger.

He offers to get me another drink, but I refuse. I'm quite buzzed enough as it is. At some point between him gesturing to the bartender, and me saying 'no', my hand brushes past his arm, only increasing the tension between us. Does he feel it too?

Despite the lights trained on us, I've almost forgotten where I am and why I'm here. Until a waitress comes up to us and invites us to make our way into the dining area. And suddenly the cameras, sound guy, and other production staff start moving along with us, reminding me of their existence again. I do hope I haven't made a fool of myself so far.

It takes them a minute to set everything up, leaving Daniel and me as helpless onlookers in a circus far bigger than just the two of us.

"This is weird, huh," I mumble.

He chuckles. "So weird."

Claire beckons us over once everyone is in place. For a brief moment, Daniel's hand ends up on my back as he guides me to my seat. It's so gentlemanly. So smooth. All my judgments from when Claire first sent me the video are forgotten. He isn't the awkward one at all. *I* am.

He starts up the conversation again, as soon as we sit down. I don't know what I was expecting really, but not this. He was visibly uncomfortable in that video I couldn't stop reviewing. Maybe because he hadn't gotten used to the cameras yet then, whereas now he's gotten more practice. Or maybe… Maybe it's the company?

"I'm sorry, what?" I stammer, upon realizing that I completely missed the last thing he said.

He smiles and leans forward. "I said, I hear the fish is really great."

I also lean in. "All this is still making me a bit nervous, if I'm totally honest."

He looks around. "It would be better without the

audience," he agrees.

I rest my elbows on the table and stay leaned forward. His eyes have captivated me again. He's so right. If there was nobody watching right now, I'd feel so much freer. I'd… what *would* I do? It would open up so many possibilities. I'd want to flirt a bit more overtly. I'd stretch my leg out just far enough for my foot to end up closer to his… I'd… I wouldn't do any of those things, because I'd still be a nervous wreck.

One of the girls working under Claire holds up a handwritten sheet of paper in my direction which reads 'family.' Claire did coach me on that. To open up a little bit and talk about Grace as soon as possible. I suppose I'll have to, but it doesn't feel natural. I'm her mother, and it's my job to protect her from all this weirdness. Then again, if I don't talk about her, how will that make her feel? Once this airs, someone will recognize me. And kids talk. Damn, do they talk. This all is bound to get back to her eventually.

"So, umm…" I train my eyes on him again. "I probably should have mentioned this sooner, but I do have a daughter from a previous relationship. I want to make sure that isn't a deal breaker for you."

Ouch, that was awkwardly shoehorned in, wasn't it? Maybe they can edit that to sound a little less… *Ugh.*

Daniel raises his eyebrows, and the corner of his

mouth twitches just a little. What does it mean? Then again, if I wasn't so shit at interpreting body language, maybe I wouldn't still be single.

"What's her name?"

"Grace… She's just… God, she's my world." As soon as I speak those words, I feel it. The warmth in my chest whenever I think of her. I'm so proud of her.

He leans forward again and stares at me with those kind eyes of his.

"Is her father still in the picture?" he asks. A fair question, even if it stings.

I shake my head. "Not really."

"Must be tough, doing it all on your own."

I wave his remark off. "You know… I spend every day doing the best I can and hope it's enough."

He's still smiling when his hand reaches across the table and lands right beside mine. I open mine, palm up, almost automatically. Just when I'm starting to wonder what the hell I'm actually doing, with all these people watching our every move, his fingers touch mine ever so softly. Not a deal breaker then? Or is this all a performance for the cameras?

Then again, Claire brought *me* in to make this look good. Not the other way around. He's supposed to be oblivious and genuinely looking for romance. I swallow hard and keep staring at our hands, carefully feeling each other out. The butterflies in my chest show no signs of calming when he finally takes my hand properly.

He's so warm. I'm so clammy. Sweet Jesus.

"I'm sure you're a brilliant mom," he says. "They say good parenting is mostly just showing up."

I've heard that being said somewhere before, but I'm still not sure what to respond. So, I just mumble thanks as I gather myself again. He still didn't explicitly share his thoughts on the matter though. And that's pretty damn important to me, no matter who all is watching.

"What about you?" I ask. "Ever thought about having a family of your own?"

Just like that, he withdraws. His hand retreats a little across the table, and the loss of our physical contact hurts almost.

"It's never been in the cards, I'm afraid," he says, then clears his throat and looks up at me again. "I mean, I've thought about it, sure, but…"

Another one bites the dust. He wouldn't want to do it with someone else's child, though. That's got to be the honest answer. Wouldn't be the first time.

"I love kids, though. They're so honest. Like, brutally honest."

He's smiling again. That boyish, almost innocent smile I've seen numerous times already throughout our short time together. It's addictive, even if he's obviously not the one for me.

"They don't know how to be any other way," I remark. In fact, Gracie wouldn't have tiptoed around any of these questions at all. She would have just bluntly asked him anything she wanted to know without fear of judgment. I guess I did manage to teach her that at least.

We're briefly interrupted by the waitress bringing our starters. Looks like carpaccio of some kind. I'm not sure how I feel about that.

Daniel waits for me to pick up my fork, then follows suit.

"Well, *bon appetit*, as they say in French."

"Yeah… that."

* Daniel *

Throughout our date so far, I've had to suppress the urge to scratch my comically short beard at least a thousand times. I've also had to really force myself to make eye contact. And remind myself to keep breathing and not just stare at her in silence.

When I finally decided to move in and hold her hand, that was something else entirely. Not at all what the me from two weeks ago would have done. Far from it. But it felt damn good, because the me from two weeks ago would have wanted to hold her hand and never mustered the courage to follow through. Guess I've learned a few things.

Still, I have no clue how to read the situation. No clue at all. I'm sure Owen will analyze it to death later on and tell me in minute detail how I could have improved every aspect of our interaction. At least that's what he did after the previous two attempts.

But yeah. Is it going well? I mean… I thought so. Until she twitched when she asked if I'd ever thought about having a family myself. As if she was trying to shake me off and get me to stay in my place. But then she smiled at me when I said I loved kids. So, maybe it *is* still going well?

This shit is hard. And even harder when you have Jill waving a sign at you from just behind your date, reading simply: 'backstory.' I get that they're here to make a television show and they want some juicy bits for the audience. And I did feel like I could make a difference by opening up about my experiences, so I didn't mind the idea initially, but…

I really like her, dammit. She's not just gorgeous and totally out of my league, but she's a mother to a little girl. The last thing she needs in her life is me and my baggage. Then again… It's old baggage.

"Actually, since you just asked if I've ever thought about having a family…"

Kate looks up from her plate. It's the patience and calm in her eyes that encourages me to complete my thoughts.

"I've never had the opportunity to consider it,

really."

"Never met the right woman?" she says.

"Something like that." Try, 'no women,' at least not in that context. No dates. No relationships. No, nothing. But that would sound pathetic and desperate, so I'm not going to be that blunt about it.

"I've had some challenges which I needed to overcome first." I shrug.

She puts her fork down and leans forward just a little. "Tell me."

Behind Kate, Jill is practically jumping up and down while gesturing at me to keep talking. This is so awkward. And not something I've had the opportunity to discuss during the previous shoots because they went so badly. It's a raw topic. Embarrassing. Then again, I don't have anything to be embarrassed about, do I? I had issues. I overcame them. This should be something to be proud of, rather than ashamed. So why doesn't it feel like it?

"My childhood wasn't great, to be honest." And that's the understatement of the century right there. My home life, and then the bullying I faced… I can't bring myself to get into detail.

This time it's her hand which creeps across the table a little, until her fingers rest next to mine. That's good, right?

"I had to do a lot of work on myself to overcome all that."

Her fingers touch mine, and vice versa. Soft, perfectly manicured fingers, so slender and elegant compared to my thick builder's hands. I look down and marvel at myself, sitting here in a scenario which would have been unthinkable not so long ago.

"Basically, I had a lot of anxiety. Depression as well… I mean, it's all under control now, but I so wish I could go back to my younger self and—"

"Tell yourself that things can get better? Yeah, I know how that feels," Kate says.

"Yeah."

"I think it's entirely human to have something like this. Some issue. Some past event. Something standing in our way. It could be small, or it could be big. But everyone has something, even if nobody else can see it, and it's still there all those years later. And you can only fulfill your potential in life if you manage to figure out what it is and how to deal with it."

I find myself nodding along with her, and caressing the side of her index finger with mine. Though I'm still raw after having to bring up my mental health issues.

"Right."

Jill is still gesturing at me. I guess they want more detail. And Kate is still looking up at me. Does she want more, too? Don't I owe it to myself to be fully open? And to others stuck in the same situation? Isn't that what I kept telling myself after the audition last month? That even if I didn't get anything out of this directly, at least I could make a difference…

"Although, for me, my issues weren't just invisible."

"No?"

I chuckle nervously and shake my head. That's when Kate places her hand on top of mine, and I close my eyes for a moment, just enjoying the sensation of her skin against mine.

"I've always struggled with my weight. And by 'struggled,' I mean, I was just out of control throughout my twenties. Over the last few years I managed to turn things around somewhat, and I know I still have some ways to go—"

"Wow," Kate says. "That's—"

Sad? Pathetic? Repulsive?

"—so inspiring!" Kate smiles at me.

Somehow it's this smile, paired with the fact that she's still got her hand on top of mine, which hits me right in my core. If our date goes south after all this, I'll be devastated.

CHAPTER FOUR

*** Kate ***

The date went so well. Better than I could have hoped for.

By the time we finish our entire three course meal, I feel like we've been friends for years. It's all him. He's a much better conversationalist than I could ever be. It's odd how he managed to meet my expectations in all the good ways, and exceed them in everything else. Most of all, despite the weirdness of having all the cameras and microphones, and crew members standing around while we had our date, I'm just glad I let Claire talk me into this.

I would have regretted it forever, had I never met Daniel in person.

Though… There is still one doubt which I'm having a hard time with. The fact that I'm a single mother. While Daniel said all the right things, I'm still not sure how he really feels about it in a romantic context.

The way he asked if her father is still in the picture. As if the presence of another man in my past poses a threat to him. It makes sense, especially because of what Claire said about him having literally no relationship experience. Maybe deep down he was hoping to be someone's first as well? That's something I could never give him.

After the meal, Nicole, the on-set stylist, takes me aside and touches up the makeup that melted off underneath the harsh spotlights.

"Nervous?" she asks.

I force myself to stop fidgeting with my hands.

"It's tough putting yourself out there as a single mom," I tell her.

She nods. "I get it. But Dan loves kids. He's really keen to have a family, he said so himself."

Sure, but most men want their own family. Not someone else's.

"He's really sweet though, isn't he? All of us on the crew really like him," Nicole continues. "More so than any of the other contestants we've had."

"I like him too," I whisper.

Nicole pauses what she's doing to my face and reciprocates the smile I didn't realize has crept over my face. "I can see that."

I exhale sharply and crack and flex my fingers to expel some nervous energy. "What's next?"

Nicole starts touching up my lipstick. "They just have to shoot the last scene. Over on the sofa." She nods towards a small cordoned off area in the restaurant with a bright red sofa taking center stage.

The name of the show, written in a very fussy cursive font, is suspended over the sofa against the whitewashed brick wall beyond: 'Sealed with a Kiss.'

So cheesy. I'd love it, if I was experiencing it all as a spectator rather than a participant.

"I can't believe Jill or Claire didn't explain this bit yet, but I've seen it often enough now…" Nicole chatters away. "You'll sit next to each other on the couch, then they'll ask both of you if you want to go on another date together, and if so, to seal it with a kiss."

"I'm supposed to kiss him? With everyone watching and a couple of cameras shoved in my face?"

"Well, I mean… Only if you feel like it!" Nicole tries to reassure me.

Somehow that's not reassuring at all.

"What if he doesn't want to? What if…" Jesus. This is ridiculous. I need to talk to Claire right now! The last thing I need is to put myself out there only to be rejected on national television.

"Relax, he's crazy about you," Nicole tells me. "Haven't you seen how he looks at you?"

I shake my head. "Where's Claire?"

Nicole points towards a cluster of people standing around just out of earshot. I excuse myself and head straight for Claire. "Do you have a minute?"

SEALED WITH A KISS

* Daniel *

As soon as we get up after our meal, I spot Owen walking towards me in his usual manner. Like he's the man behind the curtain, pulling all the strings, and the rest of us are just his pawns.

"Okay, hit me with your insights," I say. "What all did I do wrong?"

Owen observes me for a moment, then folds his arms in front of him.

"How do *you* think it went?" he asks instead.

"I think…" I take a breath. She's gorgeous, intelligent, funny, caring, and easy-to-talk-to. A mother with a young daughter. Someone who is used to having a handle on things; someone who is independent and stronger than I could ever be… "I think she's way out of my league. More so than the others. Next question?"

I may have a lot of reservations about Owen and his methods, but he has the best poker face I've ever seen. It's rather impressive how he doesn't give anything away unless he chooses to.

"Why do you say that?" he asks.

"Because it's a fact." I shrug. "Please tell me what all I messed up, so that I can apologize to her and try to fix it before she leaves here tonight."

"Daniel… We talked about this. If you want your relationships to work out, it's important to show vulnerability. Honesty. Do it in a way that doesn't come across as needy."

I frown, but I know better than to argue with the self-professed relationship expert. Vulnerability, without neediness. Got it. Just how I'm meant to accomplish that is still a mystery to me.

"So, what are you going to do next?" he asks.

Ah, the same old question they'll ask during the segment which the entire dating show takes its name from… Do I want to go on a second date? Do I want to seal it with a kiss…

My chest tightens as a fresh wave of nerves washes over me. I know this feeling very well. It's milder than it used to be, but it's still my old friend, anxiety, rearing his ugly head. Instinctively, I take a few deep breaths, exhaling slowly through my mouth until I feel myself calm down again.

"There's no way she'll do the kiss." Shit, I wouldn't kiss me in front of everyone either.

"That's not for you to think about right now. You're meant to decide for yourself," Owen reminds me. "Trying to predict another person's actions is futile. You can't control them, only yourself."

Before I get the chance to argue with him some more, Jill turns up, smiling from ear to ear.

"Daniel, that was awesome! The viewers are going to go crazy! Prepare your socials, because after this, you're going viral!"

SEALED WITH A KISS

A shiver travels down my spine. I don't want to go bloody viral. I just want… I want… I want Kate! I want nothing more than to see her again, without the damn cameras. To meet her little girl, and to get to know everything about the two of them. I want to take them for ice cream, and to go for long walks in the park. And once she puts Grace to bed in the evening, I want one of those quiet nights in, which Kate mentioned she enjoys. Just the two of us, curled up on the sofa watching Netflix or just having a good conversation over a glass of wine. And if she chooses to read all night, I want to be there with my arm around her, enjoying her presence.

Hell yes, I want a second date! But I'm not the deciding factor here. She is. Unfortunately, the format of the show is so cringe-worthy, it's sure to put her off. Seal it with a kiss? What a joke.

I don't need a kiss, certainly not on camera. I just need a chance to meet her again. Can I not have one without having to force the other?

I take another deep breath and scan my surroundings. Off to the side, near the couch where the final shot is supposed to take place, I spot her… Kate…

She really is gorgeous. The most beautiful woman I've ever seen by a comfortable margin, and that's saying something considering not just the previous dates I've had, but also the female crew members I've gotten to know over the past couple of weeks. Every single one of them is objectively attractive. And yet, nobody can compare to Kate.

Even now, while I watch her from afar, she makes my heart race and my palms sweat. She takes my breath away. Right now, though, she looks like she's arguing with Claire. This is it. This is the moment she wishes she'd never agreed to any of it.

Right from the start, there was something about her which I couldn't put my finger on. She kept commenting about the cameras, and how weird the whole situation was. I mean, sure, it's bloody bizarre. But maybe she didn't really know what she was getting herself into. She didn't pose for the camera like my other dates. She was nervous, uncomfortable.

I already know what's coming: the final scene of the episode. But maybe… Maybe nobody explained it to her until now?

She doesn't want to do it. The way she's gesturing at the sofa to Claire. She wants no part of it.

Claire rests her hand on Kate's shoulder, and Kate relaxes a little. I know that body language. She's being handled, the way Jill handled me when I nearly walked out of this circus during the last shoot.

"She won't agree," I mumble.

Owen clears his throat next to me. Has he been standing here this whole time, while I'm watching my prospects of a happy outcome crumble in front of me?

"You don't know that," he says.

"Do you think I could ask for her number regardless? Try again without the audience?" I wonder aloud.

Owen cracks a rare smile. "I think that's an excellent idea. You absolutely should. See? You *have* been listening after all!"

"Everyone!" Jill calls out somewhere closer to the lit up sofa. "We're going to shoot the final scene!"

I grudgingly make my way towards the sofa.

"Ready?" Claire asks me as I approach. I nod.

Kate presses her lips together and forces a smile. Her eyes aren't smiling. She definitely never wants to see me again after this.

Claire pats her on the shoulder, and directs Kate towards the right side of the sofa, so I automatically take a seat towards the left.

I wish I knew what to say right now. All I can do is wipe my clammy palms on my thighs and pray for this moment to end already.

Kate clears her throat beside me. "God, I'm so nervous."

Nervous? I turn to face her. She really does look scared.

"It's okay, don't worry," I tell her, though I'm terrified as well.

"All these cameras… I don't know how you're not

shitting bricks right now. Excuse the language."

Her little outburst gives me hope. "I guess I've learned to ignore them," I say before I can catch myself.

"I wish I could. Then this whole situation would be so much easier."

"Do you think we could—" I start, only to be cut off by Claire, who isn't in the mood for any further delays. Just as well. Time to rip the Band-Aid off. Third time lucky, my ass.

"Daniel, I've got a few questions for you about your date with Kate," Claire says.

Date with Kate, that's catchy. I try to suppress the nervous twitch in the corner of my mouth and nod briefly instead. She asks me to say a few words about how I thought it went; then she asks Kate the same thing. I know the drill, because I've done it before, and just say whatever pops into my head about how we like a lot of the same things and we seem to have a similar outlook. And chemistry. There was chemistry, right?

Kate fumbles a little on her answer. Is she really just nervous about the cameras? Or is she nervous because she's planning to reject me and doesn't know quite how to put it? Maybe I should do it first, avoid the entire ordeal? But then, I know Claire and Owen were aiming for a happy ending for their show. That's what we're here for. Whether or not there's a happy ending in it for my love life is secondary, or so it feels.

You're gonna go viral, Jill said earlier. Jesus. This is a lot of pressure. The whole country is going to see my downfall.

"Daniel, would you like to see Kate again and go on a second date with her?" I turn to Kate again. One look into her wide blue eyes is enough to make me forget everything I'd just been thinking about.

"Kate, do you want to see Daniel again and go on a second date with him?"

The pause between us is utterly nerve wracking. "If so, I invite you both to seal it with a kiss."

She looks up at me; her bottom lip trembles slightly. Our height difference is significant, and so it's obvious even while sitting down.

"What do you think?" I whisper, surprised at how hoarse my own voice sounds right now.

She blinks a few times, takes a deep breath, and mouths one word.

"Yes."

I smile, despite myself. Despite all the turmoil in my brain. Despite thinking only moments earlier that I should have pulled the plug on this myself. Nothing matters anymore. Because when she leans in, and wraps her hand around my neck, I'm helpless to do anything other than just go with it. I lean in too. I clumsily place my hand on her shoulder.

Her perfume takes my breath away. Or maybe it's

the sight of her, eyes slightly moist, breaths just a little too quick. The buzzing in my hand worsens the longer I carry on touching her. I'm high and mellow all at once.

I pause there, and she bridges what little distance remains between us. For a brief moment, it feels like I leave my own body and just observe the scene that's playing out between us. Her lips press against mine for a breathless kiss. It lasts only a few seconds, but those precious seconds will be branded on my memory forever.

The butterflies in my stomach. The tingling in my fingertips. The tickle of her breath against my chin… The almost inaudible little moan that escapes her lips, just before she pulls away again and looks up into my eyes.

"I'd love to go on a second date with you, Daniel," she says.

No fucking way. This is a dream, it has to be. The best dream I've ever had.

"Hell yes," I say. Just at that moment, she smiles. Once again, it's the most beautiful thing I've ever seen. I can't believe this is really happening. To *me*, of all people. And yet, here we are.

CHAPTER FIVE

* Kate *

One day you're going on a not-very-blind date as part of a reality TV shoot, the next you're back in the daily grind, wondering if it ever really happened. It's late on a Friday night; I've already put Gracie to bed. And my thoughts keep wandering back to that day… The day when I did something crazy. When I wasn't myself, but someone a lot more adventurous and uninhibited. The day I met Daniel…

I left the set late, after completing a bunch of pending paperwork, and filming a couple of segments talking about my backstory. Claire promised she'd keep the editing tight and make sure none of my many flubs and fumbles end up in the final episode. I'm going to have to take her word for it, because I don't think I'd ever want to watch it back myself. The prospect is too mortifying. I might not even tune in to the other episodes. Not while it's this raw.

Daniel and I last spoke there. On set. Before everything wrapped up and both of us went our separate ways.

Since then, two weeks of radio silence. Despite

exchanging numbers. Despite assuring each other that we did indeed want to see each other again. Was it all bullshit from his side? It didn't feel like it at the time. And yet, he hasn't called or even messaged.

And I… I suppose I could have messaged him, but I haven't mustered the courage. I guess I'm old fashioned that way. I like for a guy to make the first move. No, strike that. I'm too much of a chicken shit to put myself out there again. It's backfired one too many times in the past. That, and Evelyn has kept me rushed off my feet at work, so I haven't had a lot of mental space to formulate a plan. That's what I've been telling myself at least.

Now, so much time has passed, that it feels so alien to think back to the time we spent together. How much of it was real, and how much of it is just my memory playing tricks on me? I really did like him. A lot.

And that little kiss, as part of the final scene of the episode… I didn't want to do it, not with everyone watching… Not because I didn't want to kiss him, but because I was afraid of how it would come across. If everyone would be able to see how smitten I was. It's what I argued with Claire about just moments before I had to go on. I wanted her to promise me not to air it if it turned out too embarrassing.

And so, rather than go with the part of my gut instinct that told me to devour him, I listened to my cautious side. I gave him what was essentially a peck on the lips. It was quite tame. Quite sweet, I thought. Maybe it was too tame, too half-assed, and that's why he hasn't called? Did he think I wasn't really into him and I just gave in to peer pressure?

Or did he see me with Claire and figured out that I already knew her? I should have never promised her not to say anything. You can't start a relationship based on lies and omissions.

When my phone rings late on this Friday evening, my heart still skips a few beats though. Because for a split second, before checking the screen, I wonder if it's him. Who else would call me at this time?

Claire. Obviously.

I sigh deeply, mute the mindless chatter on TV, and settle into the sofa.

"Hey, Claire," I say.

"Kate! How are you?" she asks.

I shrug, and take a sip of wine. How am I? Overworked, underpaid, and still painfully single.

"Same old shit. You tell me?"

There's a pause. God, if she asks me for another favor right now, I'll scream.

"It's been good, actually," she says. "We wrapped up filming that night, as you know, then edits… Anyway, it's all done and delivered to the network now."

"Cool… I'm glad to hear it." What isn't she telling

me? There's something, for sure.

"They're going to start airing it in late September."

"September, huh?" I guess I'm going to stay away from live television until Christmas, just to be on the safe side. There's no way I'm going to risk tuning in, even accidentally.

"Well, anyway, I was thinking now that I'm a little free, let's have that coffee I still owe you? Give me the chance to thank you in person for saving my backside," Claire says.

I close my eyes and sigh deeply. "Gracie has a birthday party tomorrow afternoon, then I promised my dad we would visit on Sunday… I'm quite slammed, to be honest."

"Understandable. It's rather short notice…" Claire tells me.

I'm not even sure why I'm making excuses. I could very well meet up with her while that birthday party is going on. It's not like I'm expected to stick around.

"Well, what about now?" Claire asks. "What are you doing right now; busy?"

I look at the half-empty wine glass, and the silent images playing on the TV. The opposite of busy, but I'm not sure I have the energy to socialize right now.

"We could just stay on the phone, catch up, crack open a bottle of red, maybe," Claire says. "It won't be exactly like the good old days, but hey, let's make the best of it?"

SEALED WITH A KISS

I smirk at the wine glass. Well ahead of you already, girl.

"Come on, what do you say?" she urges.

I take a deep breath, and stretch out my legs on the sofa. "I've got a head start on the bottle of red wine, so you'd better catch up quick."

"I can do that."

I put the phone on speaker and lay it down in my lap while topping up my glass. Claire has a special talent to get whatever she wants. Resistance is futile. And maybe talking to her wouldn't be such a bad idea after all.

On the other end of the line, I hear the pop of a wine cork, followed by liquid being poured.

"There. We're on the same page now," Claire tells me.

"Cheers!" I raise my glass at the muted TV, and imagine Claire doing the same thing, wherever she is, before taking a sip.

"I'm sorry I didn't check in with you sooner," Claire says.

"That's quite alright. I've been super busy at work."

"Is what's-her-name still giving you a hard time?"

"Evelyn? Only every other day. Must be nice, not having a boss hovering over you every day…" I muse.

Claire chuckles. "It's not all sunshine and roses, you know? You can't imagine the drama that happens on a TV set…"

"Oh?"

"But that's a story for another day." I hear Claire take another sip before continuing. "Tell me, have you been on your second date with Daniel yet?"

I exhale sharply and shake my head. "He never called."

"He never—" Claire scoffs. "I'll be damned."

"I mean… You saw the whole thing. What did I fuck up? The conversation or the awkward kiss at the end?"

"Girl, you were perfect. You two were the absolute cutest couple I've ever seen. Just as I knew you would be."

"Apparently not," I remark dryly.

"Shit… Well, this isn't what I hoped for; I'll tell you that much."

"Yeah, me neither."

"Have you tried reaching out to him? Maybe he lost your number, or something?"

I make a face at my phone, then take another, bigger sip of wine. "I saw him type it in and save it. Then he gave me a missed call, so I'd have his number too."

Claire mumbles something unintelligible.

"What?" I ask.

"Oh, I was just thinking… This is all rather odd. Everyone who spoke to him during the shoot said the same thing. He was totally taken with you! And obviously you told me you felt the same…" Claire says.

"Well, clearly not." Or maybe… Maybe he was. Until he realized that I hadn't been upfront with him, and changed his mind then. "Hey, Claire?"

"Mhm?"

"Do you really think I should call him?"

She doesn't respond, at least not straightaway. "Kate, I think you should go with your gut on this."

My gut is telling me that if I do call him, and if we meet again, I'm going to come clean. At least then I'll know for sure that I've given it my all. But I don't tell her any of this, because I don't want her to remind me of the promise I made to her, which I'm about to break. "Okay."

"Hey, did I ever tell you what happened with the cooking show I was shooting before this?" Claire says.

I close my eyes and breathe a sigh of relief that the conversation is moving on. At least I've got a plan, half-baked or otherwise. "No, you never did. Confidentiality agreements, or some such. Which show was it again?"

I settle back into the sofa while she starts her story.

* Daniel *

For the first week after the show, I barely slept. Now, the second week is coming to an end and not a night passes without dreams. Dreams about Kate. Dreams about having a family.

Dreams about that one too-short kiss, which hit me completely by surprise.

I was so certain she would back out. That our on-camera date would end like the others. I was bracing myself for certain doom. And what I got instead nearly knocked me out.

We exchanged numbers when we chatted briefly afterwards. I told her I'd call her…

And what have I done?

Nothing.

I haven't called her. She hasn't called me. We have done nothing at all.

"Owen was wrong," I mumble.

Jack, who had been sitting beside me with his head in my lap, looks up. His big dark-brown eyes stare up at me, as if he's trying to interpret what I'm talking about. I pat him on the head and stroke his floppy ears one after the other.

"Owen has no idea, honestly. He doesn't live in reality," I say. "You, on the other hand, would never bullshit me like that!"

Jack tilts his head in that adorable way he always

does when I'm talking to him. I carry on petting him, while thinking back to last week's conversation with Owen. I'd asked Jill for his number, just in case. He didn't seem surprised when I called him. Neither did he seem surprised that I hadn't called Kate yet. But then again, he doesn't ever share his true thoughts, so perhaps he was just playing coy with his opinions as usual.

He did mention something new to me about the questionnaires I'd filled out with him prior to the first episode, about my likes, dislikes, personality traits, and expectations from a future partner. He told me that when comparing my results to Kate's, our compatibility score was off the charts high.

For a moment after our conversation, I felt a glimmer of hope. I even pulled up her entry in my contact list and considered hitting the call button for a little while. But I didn't follow through. Because I remembered what a disaster the previous dates had been, which supposedly had been set up based on the same metrics he's been trying to develop. I remembered that Owen's system, and by extension everything he's been telling me, is a pile of shit.

People lie in surveys. Hell, *I* lied in mine. Not in a big way, but I certainly answered some questions based on wishful thinking more than actual truth.

And Kate is a beautiful, responsible, independent woman. She has a daughter who relies on her. She's a lot more functional and put together than I could ever be. She's dated before, had relationships before, even had a family before.

I, meanwhile, am new to all of it. What the hell do I bring to the table? Financial stability? She has that already all on her own.

And now two weeks have passed, and along with it, any chance of a good outcome.

I fucked it up.

Mostly, I just didn't know what to say to her. I didn't know how to ask her out on a real date, without other people taking care of every little detail. What would we even chat about, without Jill and Claire giving us directions and talking points?

What if all of it was a carefully curated performance? And I fall completely flat on my own…

For all of two weeks, I've been convincing myself that maybe I need to accept the experience for what it was: A beautiful memory. A precious moment in time, which I can look back on and smile about, because nothing like it is ever going to happen to me again. I aimed too high, and got burned.

There I go with the doom and gloom again…

My finger hovers over Owen's contact details on my phone. Do I call him again? He said I'm welcome to, but I'm not sure he meant it…Then again, who else knows the situation as well as he does? Who else could give me the perspective I need?

"Daniel, how are you doing?" Owen's voice sounds professional as always.

"Hello, Owen. Still not signing up for therapy," I tell him.

"Of course not." I can't tell if he's being sarcastic or not.

"It's just… How do I even know I'm ready for a relationship?" I ask.

Jack snuggles back into my lap, and I gently rest my hand on his head and close my eyes.

"I can't tell you whether or not you're ready for a relationship. You have to figure it out for yourself."

I scoff, because obviously he wasn't just going to give me a straight answer.

"That said," Owen continues. "A good indicator would be that you're content with your life right now. You're not chasing romance to fill a hole within yourself, because that never works out in the long term."

Well, that's more of an answer than he's given me in the past. I look down at Jack, and realize that I am pretty content. Except for this nagging feeling that I need to call Kate because I'll regret it otherwise.

"I've been after companionship, more than anything. Someone to share life with, rather than someone to fix what's lacking in my life for me."

"Then you're on the right track."

"You really think so?" I ask.

"Again, it doesn't matter what I think. I have no stake in this."

"Right." I roll my eyes.

"Let me ask you something," Owen says.

"Sure."

"When you were interacting with her, did you worry about any of this stuff?" he asks.

I take a deep breath and start scratching Jack behind his left ear until his rear paw starts twitching. "I was going with the flow. Enjoying every moment with her."

"Sounds like it was easy. Effortless."

"Right," I mumble. It *was* easy. So then why is it such a monumental task just to pick up the phone and call her?

"Another thing before I hang up," Owen says.

"What?"

"She's still waiting for your call. But just how long she'll carry on waiting is anybody's guess."

I forget to breathe for a second. "She, what? You know this for a fact?"

"I have it on good authority."

My mind is racing with possibilities now. At the off chance that he's telling the truth, and not just feeding me more bullshit... Maybe I should just man up and do it. We did seem to get along well; effortlessly, as Owen said. And she literally told me she wanted to go on another date after kissing me in front of all those cameras! Jesus, I'm a bloody idiot.

"Thanks, Owen."

"My pleasure, Daniel. Remember what I've been telling you: be vulnerable. Be authentically yourself. And don't call me again until after you've reached out to her." The line clicks to signal the end of the call.

I lower the phone into my lap and stare at the darkened screen. Did he literally just give me an ultimatum? It seems so out of character, I'm almost certain I imagined it.

In any case, I should follow this instinct before it fades again. A deep breath later, I've pulled up Kate's contact details again. I count to three, and this time, I actually make the call. Here goes nothing.

CHAPTER SIX

When I enter the restaurant for my lunch date with Daniel, I'm even more nervous than I was the first time. Just why, I can't quite say. I guess there's more hanging in the balance now. More expectations which will lead to deeper disappointment, should things go wrong.

In the end I never called him; he called me the very next day instead, apologizing for the delay. Something tells me that Claire might have had a hand in it. However it happened, I haven't forgotten the decision I made that night: I'm going to come clean before we get any further into this, whatever this thing between us turns out to be.

We decided to meet at a historic gastropub overlooking Kew Gardens, not too far from my place. The food is supposed to be amazing, and the surroundings are quiet and serene.

Just like last time, he's already inside, waiting by the bar near the entrance. And just like last time, when I walk up to him, my knees are shaking and my heart is racing, and I don't quite know what to do with myself. Except smile. I'm grinning from ear to ear like the damn Joker.

"Daniel, hi!" I say.

He turns around and smiles back at me, and immediately, a sense of relief washes over me. He does look happy to see me at least. And I'm just thrilled that all of the excitement and attraction I remember from our very unorthodox first date still carries over to this moment. I'm as smitten as I was then. He gives me a brief side-hug, and I start to float.

The only thing clouding the moment of our reunion is the thing I still have to confess. The lie. Or rather, the lie by omission. And if I put it off, I'll lose my nerve entirely.

"Here, I reserved a table by the window," he tells me, while guiding me through to a part of the dining area that overlooks the carefully manicured lawns opposite the entrance to the botanical garden.

I take a deep breath and rest my hand on Daniel's arm. He pauses.

"Daniel, before we carry on, I have something to tell you."

"Yeah?"

"And I just want to say, it's okay, whatever you decide after that. If you want to postpone or even cancel our date, that's totally within your rights…" God. This is already awful, and I haven't even said anything yet. I let go of him, letting my arm hang awkwardly by my side.

"You're freaking me out. What is it?" he says, half-chuckling. His eyes are dead serious, though.

"You know how the whole concept of the show was that it was all supposed to be blind dates?"

"Yeah…" His eyes narrow slightly as he studies me.

"It wasn't a blind date for me."

There's a moment of silence between us so loaded, I feel like the entire building might fall on my head. Even the wait staff are nowhere to be seen. As if they could sense the drama unfolding between us and stayed as far away as possible.

"What do you mean, exactly?"

I make a face. "Well, I've known Claire for years; we grew up together… And when they were looking for a match for you…"

"You came on the show as a favor to her." He averts his gaze, training it on his hand, which had been holding onto the backrest of the chair he was about to pull out for me. Like the absolute gentleman that he is.

"Kind of… But not really." I'm shocked by how bad it all sounds now that I've told him. Maybe this confession was a mistake. I should have rehearsed what I was going to say!

"Well then, I guess I just have one question for you now." He makes eye contact with me again, ever so briefly. The dejection I see in his eyes sends shivers down my spine.

"Ask me anything," I whisper.

"If you went on the last date as a favor to Claire, then what are you doing here now?"

I press my lips together and take a deep breath. "Despite how all this sounds, I didn't do any of it for her. She asked me, and I initially refused. I'm quite a private person. The only reason I came onto the show was to meet you. And that's also why I came out today."

"Forgive me if I find that a little hard to believe." His voice is missing that warm edge which I found so attractive last time. He's hurt. I can't blame him.

"Believe what you want, but it's the truth. She sent me a video of you, hence why I said it wasn't a blind date from my point of view. You seemed like you'd be my type of person, which is what she was trying to tell me anyway, even when I refused her initially…"

"So you refused, and *then* she sent you a video?" he asks. The coldness hasn't gone from his eyes, nor his voice. I suppose that's to be expected. How would I react if someone had told me the same thing?

"I agreed only after I saw you on video," I confirm.

"Okay…"

"After I heard your voice, after I learned more about you. Your interests, all those things. That's when I realized I really needed to meet you."

"Well, that'll be a first," he grumbles.

"I've kept this from you because she made me promise, but I never lied about anything else I told you," I say, while reaching for his arm again. He flinches and I give up.

This has to be the hardest conversation I've ever had. By far. Harder even than everything that happened with Blake, when we were still together. In hindsight, I was never really that invested. Shocking, considering he got me pregnant. But we were young. Stupid. Reckless. Mostly, I just went along with whatever *he* wanted.

Now, I feel so much more mature and responsible. Everything I do, I reconsider a thousand times, because it's not just me who's affected. It's Gracie, too. That's why I couldn't let this secret fester between us, only to bite us in the ass later on. Especially since I've been burned before when I tried to date the last couple of years.

"I'm really sorry for deceiving you, in a way."

"Fucking Owen," Daniel scoffs and shakes his head while staring out the window beside us.

"Sorry, who?"

"The relationship expert from the show. He told me all this crap about matchmaking and personality traits and who knows what else. About how it was a totally scientific process, and it would work for everyone. And in the end, none of his shit worked out, and Claire brought you in as a charity match and they all fucking lied to my face about it."

"Ex-fucking-cuse me?" I blurt out. "Me? A charity?"

"What else? They couldn't find anyone, because his process isn't in fact as great as he thinks it is. It was starting to get awkward after a couple of failed attempts; presumably Claire told you about that as well. So, she asked you for a favor, and you agreed. It's all falling into place."

"So that's what all those questionnaires were for… I thought it was weird, so much personal information. But then, I've never been on a reality show before, so what do I know?"

"They actually had you do the surveys?"

"I thought the questions would never end."

He sighs. "Owen told me you scored higher than any of the other applicants."

"I don't know what the fuck that means," I say, still sore about his earlier comment.

"What did you get out of it, though? They promise you that you'd go viral?"

"Viral? I'm not even on social media! Why on earth would I want to go viral?" I shake my head in disbelief.

"Then what? There has to be something?" Daniel glares at me. I glare back.

If nothing else, the fact that he's pissed me off is giving me courage I wouldn't have had otherwise. That should help get the whole truth out there without stupid nerves getting in the way.

"There was. My *something* was very simple. It's actually funny considering how our conversation is going right now."

"Oh yeah? What'd you get?"

"I just wanted to meet *you*," I say.

"Yeah right."

I throw up my hands in exasperation and take a seat at the table. If this is all going to hell anyway, I might as well take the weight off my feet. I wore a pair of killer heels to try and look nice for him, but clearly, I'm letting my feet get sore for nothing.

*** Daniel ***

I'm still shaking my head, staring out the window with my arms folded, when I hear Kate pull out her chair and take a seat. She doesn't honestly think this date is going ahead as planned, is she? After everything she just told me?

She was a plant. Of course she was. It was all a trap, and I fell for it head over ass. And the audacity to get annoyed with *me* when I said it was a charity match? She's delusional, clearly.

And fucking Owen, badgering me into calling her

for this date. Why? So I could get humiliated?

"So," Kate says.

I glance over at her, while she's rubbing her calf. With me almost towering over her, and her folding herself nearly in half to stretch out her leg, I've got a rather tempting view downward into her…

No! Stop it! It was a trap then, and it's a trap now! The fact that you can see all the way down the front of her dress doesn't mean you treat yourself to an eyeful!

"What?" I ask.

"What did *you* want to get out of it?" She looks up at me. A slight tremble is visible in her bottom lip, as if she's got something more to say, but she's doing her best to keep it contained. Her eyes are still shooting daggers, though.

"Honestly?" I'm not even sure why I'm bothering to answer her. Isn't this all just a giant waste of time? I could have been at home with Jack watching a movie, or taking him out to the dog park to play fetch…

"I've been honest with you now that I've come clean. Would be nice if you'd do the same."

Has she been? All the bullshit she just told me about just wanting to meet me doesn't sound like the truth to me… But then… Unless there's a hidden camera somewhere to record us as a prank, what is she still doing here?

"I literally just wanted to—"

She straightens herself in her seat and her eyes soften the longer she looks up at me. There's something in her expression, her body language, which I can't quite identify. Something which makes me want to reach out, take her hand, and just talk to her like I managed to do during our first date. But it was all a farce!

"You wanted to—what?" she asks.

I shake my head. No, the answer that's sitting right there, on the tip of my tongue, is just too embarrassing to say out loud.

"I know that this conversation is uncomfortable. But I figured if we're going to try and make this work in real life, I'd better tell you the truth now rather than later. Relationships based on lies never last."

Is that truly what she wants, a relationship? With *me*? Why? My mind is swimming with conflicting thoughts. I think back to only moments ago, when I saw her walking into the pub. How radiant she looked, smiling brightly at me, before giving me a little hug. How my heart seemed to swell in my chest, and a pleasantly warm buzz spread through my entire body, making it feel like I was walking on clouds.

Then, once she made her confession, all of that faded until it became mere background noise. Yet it never fully disappeared…

Be vulnerable, not needy. Owen's words of supposed

wisdom continue to haunt me. *You can't control other people, only yourself.* I guess he wasn't wrong. I can't make her be honest with me; I can only try and express myself.

"I came on the show to find love," I hear myself say. Ugh, that feels awkward.

Kate's expression softens a little more. "Me too."

I pull out a chair for myself and join her on the opposite side of the table.

"I'm so sorry I didn't tell you sooner. It just felt like the kind of thing that should be explained in person." She extends her arm towards me, palm up. I take the invitation and grab her hand. Butterflies fill my chest instantly, prompting me to close my eyes just to regain my composure.

I chuckle softly. "Probably a good call that you didn't mention it on the phone, or we wouldn't have met up today..."

"Just one little request." Kate gestures with her thumb and index finger to show just how little.

"Yeah?"

"This right here..." She squeezes my hand to make her point. "*I* am not a charity."

I open my eyes and find her already staring at me. She looks fragile; I think I might even see the beginnings of tears. Fuck. I'm not ready for what that does to me. I guess that's that vulnerability Owen was talking about.

"No, you are not." I clear my throat.

"Okay," she whispers.

"Shit, you really just wanted to meet me, huh?" I ask, chuckling awkwardly. *Me!* Like, of all people!

She smiles widely through her tears and nods, before looking away from me. I'm enthralled all over again. I caress her fingers with mine; she reciprocates. Despite how today started, this moment right here is beautiful.

CHAPTER SEVEN

*** Kate ***

That almost went very wrong. My confession, although necessary, nearly resulted in our date ending before it ever started. One of the hardest conversations I've ever had. But now that it's done, I feel like a heavy burden has lifted off me. One which I hadn't even been fully aware of was there throughout our first date.

Now, everything is lighter. The sun shines brighter; the sky is clearer. The roses outside seem to bloom a little more abundantly. Even the food and drinks we order taste fresher too.

We leave the heavy emotions behind and chat about a variety of lighter topics. Things that would have been either too boring, or too awkward to discuss on camera. I tell him about my dull job and how none of it really lines up with what I wanted to become when I was little. He tells me about his cyber security business. Most of what he says goes way over my head, but I enjoy how passionate he seems about it.

"Tell me about your family," he asks after a brief

pause. "How'd you grow up?"

I avert my gaze, and try not to withdraw. He doesn't let go of my hand, which he's been holding for upwards of twenty minutes now.

"There's nothing much to say, really. Just your average working class upbringing. Only child. I couldn't wait to get out of there." I clear my throat.

With Dad always between jobs, and Mom picking up whatever work she could at a nearby supermarket to make ends meet, things were tough. No wonder they didn't have the happiest marriage and kept fighting whenever they thought I'd gone to sleep. Until that fateful morning around my fifteenth birthday which changed everything. I try to shake off the nastiness of that memory and look up into Daniel's eyes to ground myself again and force a smile.

"You?" I ask.

His fingers gently stroke my hand. The thoughtful expression on his face suggests that he's been listening, but also swept up in memories of his own past. He'd hinted at difficulties he needed to overcome during our first date. A part of me wants to ask for more details, but we hardly know each other well enough yet for all this. It's too sore. Too intense. These are certainly not second date conversations.

"I was an only child too," he says. "My parents had their share of issues. The fact that I kept getting in trouble in school didn't help any."

I catch myself chewing on my bottom lip. We need a change of topic, and quick.

"I'm so glad we could do this today," I remark, while caressing his hand as well. It's nice to focus just on our physical connection for a moment. The butterflies in my stomach are back in full force today. Clearly, the attraction I feel towards him wasn't just a fluke. I wonder how today's date will end. Another peck on the lips, maybe more? The longer I look at his face, the more I want. If only he wants it too…

When he catches me staring at him, his serious expression breaks into a cautious smile.

"I almost didn't call you at all," he confesses.

I press my lips together and keep quiet. That little statement from him ignites a million nagging questions. Why so serious?

He turns and gazes out the window. The fact that he doesn't let go of my hand is the only thing keeping me from panicking completely right now.

"I just wasn't sure, you know…"

Wasn't sure he liked me that way? Wasn't sure he wanted to get involved with a single mom? Just like that, the butterflies I felt morph into a hornet's nest of self-doubt. I wish I wasn't so absolutely desperate for his approval. It's actually pathetic.

"I'm really bad at this." He smiles at me briefly, then looks outside again.

"That's okay," I hear myself say, even though my anxiety is still through the roof.

"I wanted to call you the very next day, but then I thought, no, that's too soon," he says.

I take a deep breath to calm myself. I would have loved it if he'd called me the next day. That would have shown me that he's as invested as I am.

"Then, on the second and third day, I was still telling myself that the time wasn't right. And by the fourth day…" Daniel's voice trails off.

Sounds like nerves. Could it be so simple?

"What changed your mind?" I ask.

"When I said I'm bad at this, I meant that I actually don't have a clue," Daniel explains.

"Yeah." I know what he means, because Claire told me. And it's fine. I just don't know how to make that clear to him without sounding patronizing about it. Claire probably should have kept her mouth shut in the first place; those weren't her things to share.

"I knew dating would be complicated, I just wasn't prepared for all the, you know—" Daniel makes an all-encompassing gesture, then runs his hand through his hair and smiles awkwardly.

He's as tense as I was before my confession at the start of our date. And that's in equal parts heartwarming and nerve wracking.

"It's normal to be nervous," I say, noting that my own voice is trembling too now. I guess I need to hear that statement as much as he does.

"There's so much dating advice out there; so many unwritten rules."

"I'm pretty bad at following those rules. That's why I told you what I told you earlier, rather than keep you in the dark," I say.

He looks at me, and I look at him. And just like on every other occasion we've shared some eye contact, I'm lost again. God, I wish we could skip past the weirdness and just be comfortable. We seemed to be able to do that every so often during our first date, in front of all the cameras. Why should it be harder now, when we're alone? If we can just stay away from all the messy emotional topics long enough to find our footing, all will be fine.

"Okay, no rules, then?" he asks.

I think for a moment. This is a weird conversation, probably because I've never been asked to define my expectations like this before. But it's also refreshing.

"Well, I mean, I like it when a guy holds the door for me, takes my coat, or pulls out a chair," I say, referring to what he was trying to do earlier. "And I was definitely waiting for you to call, rather than ask you out myself."

Daniel smiles. "I can definitely do the former. And the latter, well, it took me a while, but I got there."

"And…" I look around, hoping for some visual cue to remind me of everything my mind has chosen to forget when he smiled at me again.

"The three day rule is out, though?" he asks. "Playing hard to get?"

"Yeah, no. Those things just feel like stupid games teenagers play." As well as every other guy I've ever tried to date. Guess that's why I'm single. I take a deep breath and look up into his eyes. "I'd much prefer it when a guy makes it very clear what he wants. And I'm willing to do the same. Just being honest, you know?"

Daniel smiles and squeezes my hand. "I like that. Being honest. It's so much easier than trying to interpret little hints and signs."

"Right? Life's complicated enough as it is."

We're lost in each other's eyes again for a moment. So much so, I barely notice when the waitress brings over our dessert and places it on the table between us.

Shit, I really like him. I knew it from the moment I saw his video. It was confirmed to me during our first date. And now… Now, I fear I'm hopelessly lost, even though I barely know him yet. This has always been my problem. When I fall, I fall quickly and hard. Mostly to my own detriment, because I'll latch on and they run. I simply don't know how to protect myself from my own tendencies.

But Daniel is different, isn't he? More mature, somehow. More present. If our conversation just now isn't proof of that, I don't know what is.

SEALED WITH A KISS

* Daniel *

This vulnerability thing Owen has been talking about is damn awkward, at least at first. But the way she's looking at me now makes up for all the discomfort of stumbling through the first half of our conversation about our dating expectations.

And when she looked me in the eye and said she prefers it when a guy just says what he wants… Jesus, that just about made me forget myself. Was the subtext in her statement intentional? Or am I trying to hunt for deeper meaning where there isn't any again?

But then… We're still holding hands. Whenever I steal a glance at her, I find that she's doing the same. And when the dessert neither of us ordered arrives at the table, complete with two spoons to share it, she picks up hers without hesitation.

We're doing this, then? Sharing food from the same plate?

The scene is straight from a romantic movie. Exactly the sort of thing I wondered if I'd ever experience. And now that I'm here, I barely know what to think.

On the one hand, I'm on cloud nine. I'm sitting here with this beautiful woman, who could literally have any man she wanted. On the other hand, I'm… well, I'm still me. I might look different now than I did a few years ago. I might have developed myself professionally, made a name for myself in the cyber security field, and even founded a reasonably successful business. But whenever I look in the mirror, I still see… *Me.*

The awkward fat kid who never had any friends growing up, only enemies. The young man who tried to fill the emptiness in his life with food and videogames until things got completely out of control. I've come a long way towards accepting myself and turning my life around, but I'm not quite there yet.

I'm sitting here, opposite this amazing goddess, who claimed earlier she actually just wanted to meet me. That's bizarre, because, who the hell am I, really? Nicole cleaned me up to get me camera ready and I've kept the same style since, but I'm still nothing special. Awkward, nervous, still about fifty pounds away from a normal BMI. Not like Kate, who might as well be Wonder Woman, as far as I'm concerned. And the fact that I'm thinking about her in superhero terms shouldn't count in my favor either.

"This looks amazing," Kate says, gesturing at the layered chocolate mousse cake on the plate in between us.

"It does." More so, because I've worked damn hard to get my sweet tooth under control these past few years by avoiding temptation. Still, I pick up my spoon to share this moment with her.

"Enjoy!" She smiles brightly, then digs in for her first taste. "Holy shit, that's delicious," she blurts out a split second later.

I follow suit. It's as amazing as she says. Everything I read about this restaurant before suggesting it as a setting for today turned out to be true. Maybe I don't need Jill and the rest of the production team to set up a halfway decent date after all.

"What's funny?" Kate asks, pausing with her empty spoon halfway between her mouth and the plate.

"I was just thinking, I love your enthusiasm, your—what's the phrase? *Joie de vivre.* "

She smiles again, which lights me up all the way from the inside out. "I can't help it. This place is just…" She gestures at the beautiful views outside. "I can't believe I've never come here before. It's not even that far for me."

"Maybe it can be our special place, then?" I blurt out.

She sits back and stares at me. "Yes, our special place. I like that a lot."

Remembering what she said about a guy honestly expressing himself, I quickly add: "All the more special because of the company."

The look in her eyes softens. It's as if I can watch her melt in front of me. It's a powerful feeling, and also completely disarming. All that stuff Owen has been trying to tell me, I guess it's finally sinking in. If exposing these awkward gooey parts of myself makes her react like this, I can't really argue with his wisdom.

"After this, do you want to explore Kew Gardens a little?" I suggest.

She purses her lips while stealing another glance outside. "I'd love that. Yes."

We share a smile, and enjoy a few more spoonfuls of our dessert; one for her, then one for me, then one for her again…

Somewhere next to my leg, I feel a certain presence, a warmth. I move my foot ever so slightly to one side, only to find her leg already waiting. She doesn't flinch or back away, she just carries on smiling, and slowly but surely cleaning her half of the dessert plate. My heart is racing and all my senses are on high alert now.

We've talked and shared more of ourselves; we've held hands. Now our feet are seeking each other out underneath the table, while our eyes can't bear to look away for more than a moment at time. Attraction, flirtation… So this is what it's like.

Assuming the rest of the afternoon goes equally well, I'd be an idiot if I don't call her right away for a third date.

CHAPTER EIGHT

*** Kate ***

I'm in love. In hindsight, I realized it when we shared that first, very tentative kiss towards the end of our first date. But now...

The magnetism between us is off the charts. We finish our dessert, and Daniel pays, despite my offer to split the bill. Meanwhile I'm giddy like a schoolgirl having her first real crush. And Daniel... I can see my own attraction mirrored right back at me whenever I look him in the eyes. Weird as it was, I'm glad we had that discussion earlier, when he asked me about all the bullshit supposed dating rules you see repeated everywhere. I don't believe in any of that crap, and if he tried to follow even half of them, it would only make me doubt his intentions.

It was certainly a more comfortable topic than the messy family stuff I narrowly avoided talking about before that. There's no way I'm going to ruin what we have together by opening that Pandora's box.

We get ready to leave for our stroll through Kew Gardens, and he opens the door for me just as I knew he would. I love it.

As we make our way past the ticket booth and through the entrance to the garden, the only thing ruining the moment for me is my choice of footwear. It's a chore, trying to walk a gravel path in a pair of stilettos.

Daniel offers me his arm. "You okay?"

I smile awkwardly and glance down at my extremely cute and equally uncomfortable heels. "They're not walking shoes, but I'll manage."

The sun is shining high in the sky, its pleasing warmth penetrating deep into my skin. That's lessening the ache in my calves, but only slightly. As we carry on past the lush green lawns bordered with colorful summer blooms, I find myself longingly gazing at the cool grass.

"Why don't you, you know…" Daniel starts.

I pause, trying desperately to look casual despite the growing pain in my feet.

"Just take them off?"

I glance up at him, then at the grass again. "It would be nice, just walking barefoot on the grass," I comment.

"It would be," he confirms.

"Well, then, let's both do just that." I smile brightly at him, and he smiles back. Within moments, we've occupied the nearest bench, where I've quickly unclasped and kicked off my shoes, while he's still busy with his laces and socks. It's a little silly what we're doing, but that only makes me feel more comfortable with him.

We might have both put in an effort to dress up for our date, but the end goal in my mind is to get to a point where we don't have to. To accept each other just how we are. I glance over at him, as he's neatly folding up his socks and stuffing them in his shoes. Can I imagine this man in bed next to me in the morning? Or in the bathroom brushing his teeth, while I do my make up before work? Would it be as effortless as it is right now?

"What are you smiling at?" he asks. He doesn't ask in an accusatory tone like the guys that came before. There's a warmth in his voice which manages to put me right at ease. Maybe the twinkle in his eye has something to do with it as well.

"Nothing, just checking out your feet," I tease. They're pretty big feet, but I keep that observation, as well as any naughty conclusions, to myself.

"Oh, is that what we're doing now? Checking out each other's feet?" he asks.

"Might as well. You've already seen mine." I wiggle my toes to make my point.

I jump up from the bench, strappy heels in hand, and let out a sigh of relief when taking my first few steps on the lawn. "This feels so good!"

"So good indeed. You know, I don't think I've ever done this before," he remarks.

"You don't go to parks generally?" I ask.

"Oh, I do all the time. But the types of parks I go to with Jack… Let's just say there are too many unpleasant surprises hidden in the grass."

I raise an eyebrow. "Who's Jack?"

"Wait, I never told you about Jack?" He turns to face me, a wide grin on his face.

He's so handsome when he smiles.

"Well, he's about two feet tall, brown with white spots, floppy ears, and the cutest little face you will have ever seen."

"Aw, I love dogs!" I say.

Daniel pulls his phone out of his pocket, and shows it to me after unlocking the screen. The wallpaper is a close-up of Jack's face, which indeed is pretty much the cutest I've ever seen.

"That's adorable," I coo. "What breed is he?"

He shrugs. "I'm not quite sure. He was a rescue. But in many ways he saved me, rather than the other way around."

I'm not sure what that means exactly, and I'm not about to pry for fear of heading for another uncomfortable conversation. I think we've had our share of messy emotions for the day.

"Do you have any pets?" he asks.

I shake my head. "I got a goldfish for Grace once, but that quickly turned into a tragedy. Between work and all the extracurricular stuff she gets up to, there isn't a lot of time to manage a pet. She loves animals, though…"

I steal a glance at Daniel, wondering if my mentioning Grace bothers him at all. But I suppose if this thing between us is going to work, he'd better understand that she is my universe. Everything I do is for her.

He puts his phone away again. "Well, Jack is really good with kids, so that's not going to be a problem, then."

I smile and slip my hand into the crook of his arm and we start walking across the lawn towards a little hillock with a giant chestnut tree.

"I mean, whenever you think it's the right time, of course," he adds.

"Thanks for understanding," I whisper.

The grass feels so soft and pillowy and just cool enough to offset the warmth of the sun. It's a perfect day. A perfect date. The perfect man? It's probably too soon for that assessment, but my heart is already five steps ahead of my rational brain.

"Wow, look at that view!" I point at the sprawling greenery extending out ahead of us. Trees and shrubs dot the grassy landscape; every shade of green is represented. Nestled in between the greenery are some of the pavilions and other historic buildings that have been here seemingly forever. In perfect harmony. Just like us?

We pause for a moment, just taking it all in. The fresh air, the buzz of excitement that has been filling my chest pretty much throughout most of our time together today. I'm not going to let anything get in our way now.

I turn to look up at him. He really is tall; more so now that I'm no longer wearing heels. Tall and broad and cuddly, with the kindest face I've ever seen. Our eyes meet and I'm lost once more.

Can he feel this too? I can't stand not knowing for sure.

My arm reaches for his shoulder, almost with a mind of its own. As soon as I touch him there, something in him changes. Something fundamental. Even the look in his eye… It's softer, like he's letting his guard down for me.

Does he like me as much as I like him? I'm afraid to ask, but still compelled to find out by touch.

His arms end up on my back, surrounding me in a reassuring embrace. It gives me just enough courage to continue. I get up on my tippy toes, while he leans down in my direction.

This is the moment. The moment of truth.

No cameras; no onlookers. We're alone in our own little bubble. Far away from everything else.

Nothing matters. Only his lips, which tentatively touch mine, just as I wrap my arms around his neck. He keeps me steady, as if he knows how badly my knees want to tremble. I smile against his lips, just as we go in for our first real taste.

This time it's unprompted. There's no pressure. Our next date doesn't depend on this, and yet it absolutely does.

I try to let go of all the thoughts that plagued me the last time. What will people think; what will Gracie think? This kiss, our first *real* kiss, is just for us. It's a perfect culmination of everything we've experienced up to this point.

He overwhelms me, in the best possible way. Takes my breath away, while simultaneously making me feel safer for it. Who needs oxygen, anyway?

Our tongues tease at each other, through half opened lips. We're feeling each other out, testing each other. *Do you like me too? Just as much as I like you?*

The answer is yes. A thousand percent yes. I can feel it in my heart with every breath.

Here I am, sensible old me, mother first and woman second, absolutely lost in the moment. Swept away by sensations I haven't felt in… possibly forever. Because I don't recall it ever being this intense. What I had with Blake before Grace was born was my first proper relationship, and kissing him never made me feel anything close to this. And any dates I went on after…

I love you, my heart seems to say. *God, I love you already.*

Thankfully I have the presence of mind not to blurt it out and send him running for the hills as well. Desperation is a bad look.

And yet… I see that same depth of emotion in him every time he briefly opens his eyes to look at me. It's those repeated glances, however brief, which give me the courage to caress his face and run my fingertips across his neatly trimmed beard. To squeeze his shoulder and pull him against me as tight as I can and touch his hair.

And in turn, he starts to move as well. His firm embrace softens; his hands gently caress the bare skin on my shoulders and arms. It strikes me how careful he is. How deliberate. I wonder if he'll be like this in bed too?

Am I seriously considering getting intimate on the second date? I would never!

Never say never, my inner voice tries to tell me. *We're all alone; no one else needs to know.*

He pulls away briefly, eyes averted.

"Stop me any time," he whispers.

I shake my head and tighten my arms around his neck to draw him back in, stumbling backwards a few steps until my back hits the rough bark of the tree. He follows, his significantly larger body pressing into me, sandwiching me between him and the trunk.

It's even more intoxicating. My knees would surely give way, if I didn't have this support behind me.

He devours me. That's the only word for it. Just as I'd wanted to do after our first date, but I was too hung up on who's watching and what-does-it-all-mean. He conquers me with his mouth. My lips, my neck; even a particularly sensitive spot near my clavicle which I didn't know would make me feel this way.

I'm ready to surrender. To give myself to him. Whatever he wants. Whatever *I* want, rather. Because this isn't just for him. This is something selfish. Something precious I want just for me. The whole world be damned right now. I want him.

* Daniel *

Never in a million years did I see things turning out quite like this. The date started off precarious, in danger of ending before it ever even started. I nearly cut things short when she told me her truth, and it would have been the biggest mistake of my life.

Even when I suggested we go for a walk in the gardens, I didn't see things progressing quite like this. Frankly, I don't even know how it came about.

One moment we were walking barefoot across the lawn, the next we're making out against a tree like a bunch of hormonal teenagers.

Surely that's all it is. Hormones. Biology.

I can't explain it any other way.

The way her every touch sets me on fire. How it took every ounce of self-control to pause for a moment to try and tell her it's okay if she wants to stop. Only for her to pull me back in for more.

Where do I go from here? What do I do?

Overwhelmed by sensations I've never felt before, except maybe in some forbidden dream.

After all the conversations I've had with Owen about love and relationships, I never really expected I'd end up here. In this tangled web of emotions. So swept up in instinct, I don't even really care if I'm doing this right.

This is my first time.

My first proper kiss.

With Kate.

Even if nothing happens after this, even if this is all I'll ever be allowed to do… It's still so much more than I deserve. So beautiful. So intense.

I could cry if I stopped and really thought about it. Luckily she doesn't give me time to, because that would surely ruin everything.

Just the way her breaths have changed—more urgent and impatient somehow—spurs me on to explore more of her. To show her how I feel about her in every way I can think of.

To love her. Body and soul.

Is that what this is? *Love?* Or is this just lust?

Somehow the word feels wrong to even consider.

Because I've felt lust before. From afar. In my imagination. And it was nothing like this.

Can she feel it too? Surely, this is all much more normal for her. After all, it's not *her* first time for any of this. She's already experienced so much more in her life. For her it's just a kiss, whereas for me…

I'm going to get burned… I'm going to—

She looks up at me, runs her hand through my hair. It makes me feel noticed. *Seen.* I am the chosen one.

"I don't normally do this…" she whispers.

Yeah, me neither.

"I want to see you again. Soon." For a split second, something changes in her eyes. I recognize it as insecurity, because I have bucket loads of my own to compare it to.

"Yes." I had to force the word out. Not sure I could say much more than that even if I wanted to.

She smiles against my lips. It's the most beautiful thing, because I already know how radiant she looks when she smiles.

I can only think to kiss her in response. Can't get enough of her. Of the sweet taste of her mouth. The subtle perfume that clings to her hair. The softness of her skin.

That too could make me cry. Like the song. *Creep.*

How the fuck is she here with me? In *my* arms, not someone else's. Someone more deserving. Someone who can be everything she needs; who *belongs* .

What am I supposed to do now? What's next?

In the movies, the guy might ask if she wants to go somewhere more private. Oh, the subtext attached to those words. I could never. Not because I don't want to. But what if she takes offense?

Worse still, what if she agrees? And I'll have to follow through on so much more I don't know anything about. No, I couldn't possibly. This will have to do for now. Until I know what's what.

"After today," she mumbles against my mouth in between further kisses.

"Mhm?"

"Don't wait two weeks to call me."

CHAPTER NINE

*** Kate ***

Life is back to normal, but I'm still obsessing about my second date with Daniel. Mostly, I just can't get *him* out of my head. He kept his word and called me. Immediately. And we've been chatting every night since and messaging throughout the day before that. About work and life and everything in between. There's always something to talk about. And he's genuinely interested in hearing about my day, which is a shocker. I've never had that. Certainly not with Blake, who in his own words never had time for my bullshit because he had plenty of his own.

As a result, I'm distracted. All day, every day. I've tried not to let work get affected, but I can't honestly say I've succeeded. Still, I remain way more productive than most of my colleagues put together. That has to count for something.

"So, those documents I left on your desk yesterday for you to summarize..." Evelyn impatiently taps her foot on the floor to make her point. Yes, on a Tuesday evening, well after five. *Those* documents. Extra work to be completed on top of my regular responsibilities. As if I don't have a life outside of this place.

"Yeah. I had that parent-teacher meeting at Grace's school which I told you about. It ran late, so I'm still working on it," I tell her.

"Right. Life happens for all of us. Doesn't mean we neglect our work." As hard as I try not to let her tone get to me, it does. Because this isn't *my* work. It's hers, which she always tries to palm off on me, before taking credit for it herself.

I take a deep breath and focus on happier thoughts. On Daniel, who's undoubtedly going to call me again later, after I put Gracie to bed. "I'll have everything finished within the hour."

Evelyn huffs angrily, but doesn't say a word. The way her nostrils flare says it all, really.

I take a deep breath and hold it, while watching her walk away. Stupid cow. Karma is a thing, right? Sooner or later this will blow up in her face and she'll get what's coming to her, surely?

Or maybe things are going to carry on exactly how they have been. Because it seems to pay off to cheat. That's why she's in charge, and I'm not.

That's also why Blake has been able to weasel out of paying his child support. Not that I need a penny from that prick. I've been able to give Gracie everything she needs all on my own, thank-you-very-much. But the fact there hasn't even been a birthday card in years, that's what's truly despicable.

Breathe in deeply. Hold. Exhale slowly. Repeat. Some people suck; what's new?

I shake my head and try to focus on Evelyn's work. The sooner I get it done, the sooner I can complete my own packed to-do list for today. So. for the rest of the day, I do my best to keep my head down, finish what I need to, and stop obsessing about Daniel so much.

No matter how persistently glimpses of us making out like randy kids under that chestnut tree try to infiltrate my mind.

God, that was hot, though. If he'd given any indication that he wanted to go further, I don't know where it would have ended…

No, strike that. I do know. My subconscious has been exploring all the possibilities in explicit detail every night in my dreams.

Rather than dump all my frustration with Evelyn on him when he calls later, maybe I should steer the conversation in a flirtier direction… I catch myself getting lost in all the potential outcomes of such a phone call, and try to get back on track.

Work first, dammit! Finish your work first!

* Daniel *

It's been a few days since our second date. And I can't stop thinking about it. About *her*.

There have been more dreams, most of which I remember in shocking detail come morning. That's unusual. I don't normally remember what I dream about.

And for the first time in I don't know how many years, I've woken up with the evidence of said dreams still very much present in my pajamas... It's my teenage years all over again, except this time I'm fantasizing about a real person I'm having an actual relationship with. I'm uncertain if that makes it better or worse. And so I've resorted to cold showers in the mornings, trying to get the morning wood under control. Because taking care of the matter at hand in any other way has felt too... Dirty.

She's a person, after all. Not some sex object. A beautiful, attractive, kind-hearted, and caring woman. A mother. Who deserves better than this. Better than me.

I've tried assuaging my guilt by sending her sweet messages in the morning to let her know she's on my mind. Because she is. Every waking moment, and most non-waking ones too. My attraction for Kate is bordering on obsession. And although I haven't attempted it, a day without speaking to her at least once would be painfully incomplete.

As tempting as it was to call Owen after to discuss everything that happened, and ask for advice on how to handle the moral dilemma I'm caught in, I decide against it for now. It's too embarrassing. And I need to figure things out on my own for once.

Instead, every time I wonder what's going on between us, I skip the go-between and call Kate directly. And conversation has flowed effortlessly every time.

That's promising, isn't it? Initially I worried that we'd run out things to talk about, but the opposite has happened. We always find something. And I always find myself smiling by the time I get off the line with her. Smiling, and feeling lighter as a result.

Effortless.

She makes me want to be a better man. To live up to her expectations. That's another thing Owen hinted at once about relationships. That good relationships make you want to become a better version of yourself. Now if I could just convince my body that she's not to be objectified, that would be great. Maybe in time, once the newness wears off.

We already fixed our next date for Saturday. Grace has a play date planned at a friend's house, giving us a few hours of alone time at a nearby coffee shop.

I understand Kate's wish to keep her daughter out of our relationship for now. At the same time… her reluctance worries me. Maybe she never intends to introduce us? Maybe deep down she realizes I don't have what it takes to become part of her family. I've thought about asking her, but something prevents me from doing so. It just feels… inappropriate.

"Don't you look at me like that!" I tell Jack, who's been staring at me for the better part of ten minutes. "I know *you* like me, but you're a dog, so what do you know about human relationships?"

He cocks his head to the side in that adorable manner of his, and I can't help but smile.

Shit, if Kate saw me talking to Jack like this, she'd think I've lost my mind.

I suppose I *have* lost my mind. I lost it somewhere in Kew Gardens, when I let instinct take over and we made out. I lost it when I let circumstance convince myself that that was the right thing to do. That I'd had some kind of a right to touch her that way. I took things too far, which is also why I'm so obsessed with her.

No wonder she wants to keep me away from her kid. Maybe she thinks I'm only after one thing? And while she seemed receptive to it in the moment— she's a grown woman with her own physical needs, after all—she doesn't see us going anywhere serious in the long term. Maybe then, the answer is to pull back on the physical a little bit to convince her that there's more between us. Real, long term stuff.

And anyway, if the next time we're alone together we end up with our hands all over each other again…

God, as tempting as that is… I'm bound to make a fool of myself sooner or later. And at the latest once our clothes come off, she'll realize that she deserves so much better than me. That's one thing the dreams and fantasies haven't been able to answer for me. How to deal with *that*.

There are some things regular visits to the gym have not been able to fix for me. I mean, I've reached a point where I look somewhat okay with my clothes *on,* but beyond that?

Just like that, Jack jumps up into my lap and starts licking my face.

"Stop it!" I complain. But his antics make me smile anyway.

"What do you want, anyway? You want to go out for a walk now? Is that what this is all about?"

The word 'walk' has the same effect as usual. Jack freezes and tries to hypnotize me. And then he jumps down off the sofa and waits in the doorway, looking back at me to see whether I'm getting up yet. Fine. I guess we're going for a walk early today. Probably a wise idea to walk more, considering I'm going to be eating out more regularly with Kate now as well. I wouldn't want to slip into old habits and make a bad situation worse.

I head for the hallway and start putting on my

shoes, while Jack excitedly bounces up and down in circles around me. He's already fetched his leash and is holding it in his mouth, ready for me to put it on.

"Settle down and be a good boy," I tell him.

That gets him even more excited. I can't help but laugh. He literally is the best.

I hook the leash on his collar and straighten back up, catching a glimpse of myself in the mirror as I do so.

While I'm not where I want to be, I've come a long way. A very long way.

Only a couple of years ago, the reflection that would look back at me looked so very different. In those days, I wouldn't have dreamed of wearing lace-up sneakers like this. It would have been impossible for me to put them on and tie the laces while standing up. There's no way I would have been able to go on these dates. No way she would have accepted.

Kate doesn't know the details of my history. While I hinted at my struggles during our on-camera date, she couldn't possibly understand. Claire and the rest of the team never even heard the worst of it.

Shit.

Kate doesn't know *me* at all.

And they're going to start airing the first episodes later this month. The ads and teasers have already begun. Claire made it pretty clear that they're going to bring my backstory into it. It's the main reason I got selected. They'll show my old photographs for sure. Kate's going to see, and she's going to wonder why I didn't tell her earlier...

Fuck.

Our last date started with Kate's confession, it's only fair that our next date starts with mine. She already doesn't want to introduce me to her kid, and after that? Who knows if she'll even want to see me again. I can't even blame her. Kids need healthy role models, and I'm... Well, past me is the exact opposite of that. And present me is still a work-in-progress. *And only a few bad decisions away from slipping back into old habits.*

Like she said last time. Honesty is vital. I owe her the truth. Wherever it may lead.

CHAPTER TEN

*** Kate ***

Despite everything, I manage to get out of the office at five-fifteen, so I'm still on time to pick up Gracie from day care. What I am, though, is exhausted. And so we swing by Tesco's on the way home to pick up a frozen pizza. It's not the healthy, wholesome meal I'd be feeding her in an ideal world. But my world isn't ideal. And at least it's a veggie pizza, so she's getting *some* nutrition out of it.

She's also super excited about it, and that's infectious.

"So next week, Ms. Lawson said we have to bring in something for show & tell. And Lucy said she'll bring in her hamster, cage and all. And I don't know what to bring…"

"We'll figure it out," I tell her, while brushing an errant lock of hair out of her face.

"All the other kids have pets… Why don't we have any pets, Mom?"

I take a deep breath, remembering the drama that unfolded when the goldfish I got her for her fifth birthday died, just two weeks later. That despite the fact that fish were supposed to be relatively low maintenance. "I'm sure not *all* the other kids have pets."

"Pretty much. Most of them. Lucy has a hamster; Sarah has a cat; Caroline has *two* dogs. Two! Why can't *we* get a dog, Mom?"

"It's a lot of responsibility, you know. Feeding them, cleaning up after them, taking them for walks multiple times a day..."

"I can do it. I promise, I'll do everything!"

I smile and shake my head. She says that now. But what happens in a couple of months when the newness wears off and she gets obsessed with the next shiny thing? With my work schedule, there's no way I could take care of a dog on top of it all. Doggy daycare isn't cheap.

"Tell you what. We could go to the zoo on Sunday, what do you say? Visit all the animals there first. Those are way cooler than Caroline's dogs."

"Really? I love the zoo!" Gracie chirps.

I can't help but smile. Thankfully this distraction still works. But I know we're going to be revisiting the dog conversation again soon. Luckily, we get through pizza, the obligatory re-watch of *Frozen*, including her dance performance, and our bedtime routine without further mention of it.

And so, once Gracie is safely tucked in, I find myself eyeing my phone, waiting for Daniel's call.

Then I catch myself. Why don't I call him first tonight? I'm already smiling when I dial his number. It barely rings before he answers.

"Hi!" I say.

"Hi, Kate!"

"I got free early today."

"No homework?" he asks.

Clearly I've been venting too much. He already knows how much I work after hours, and we've only been talking regularly for a few days.

"Not tonight." I mindlessly start to chew on my nails, when I stop myself. "Actually, she gave me a hard time today because I hadn't finished yesterday's work quickly enough for her liking."

"But you had that parent-teacher meeting?" he asks.

"I told her that. She didn't care."

"You do too much. They're taking advantage of you."

I press my lips together. I wasn't going to go down this rabbit hole, and now I've done it again.

"Never mind all this; what's going on with you?"

"Oh… Just came back from walking Jack."

"Oh, Gracie wants a dog now. Can you believe it?" I chuckle briefly, then bite my bottom lip, realizing that I'm talking myself into a worse hole now. From venting about work, to bringing Grace into things, rather than sticking to my initial plan of focusing on the two of us and trying to flirt with him. Wow, no wonder my previous dating attempts failed so miserably. I can't seem to stay on track!

"My dog is your dog, as they say," Daniel says.

"It's as if she knows," I mumble to myself. *Wait, what did he just say?*

"As if I know what?" Grace speaks up behind me. I immediately freeze and nearly drop the phone for good measure.

"Shit," I mumble. "Daniel, I'm going to have to call you right back."

"You said shit!" Grace giggles. "And who's Daniel?"

I rush to hang up the call and turn around, only to see Grace in her favorite pink pajamas, clutching Ed the octopus to her chest. Her blonde hair is all tousled, but her eyes look as alert as ever.

"I'm sorry, that's not a nice word to say," I tell her. "What happened, how come you're up and out of bed this late?"

She keeps looking at me inquisitively. Clearly she's not going to let me distract from her question with my own.

"Daniel is…" I start.

She raises her eyebrows expectantly.

"He's a man I met recently." I want to follow it up by saying he's a friend, but that feels… *Ugh. Special* friend, maybe?

"Is he your boyfriend?" Grace asks, while chewing on her lips. "Ms. Lawson has a boyfriend too. His name is Roy. They're going to get married now."

"That's… I mean…" I take a deep breath. I suppose he is. But the term sounds too juvenile for my liking.

We stare at each other in silence for a minute, then she presses her cheek against Ed the octopus and glances at the kitchen.

"I couldn't sleep. I'm so thirsty."

"Okay, let me get you some juice." I get up and start walking towards the fridge, forgetting all about my usual rule of no sugary drinks after her teeth are brushed. This line of questioning has put me off balance completely.

"Remember when I told you a while back how grown up relationships are really complicated?" I ask.

"When Lucy's parents got divorced…" Grace says thoughtfully.

"Right. Well, Daniel is really nice, but I've only just met him, so I don't know—"

"If he's nice, then what's complicated? Lucy told me her parents were always fighting. They weren't nice to each other, ever."

It sounds pretty simple, put like that. Unfortunately, life hardly ever turns out to be simple. I pour out a small glass of juice and hand it to her.

"Do you want to marry him? Like Ms. Lawson and

her boyfriend?" Grace asks, then takes her first sip.

I can't help but smile at her question, or rather, her innocence in asking it.

"If I decide that I do, you'll be the first to find out. Deal?" I ask.

She takes another sip, then puts her glass down and looks up at me again. "But how do we know he's going to be nice to me too? You can't marry someone who isn't nice to me!"

I put my arm around her and pull her against me. She hugs me back, with her stuffed toy trapped in between us. "I would never marry anyone who isn't nice to you. I promise. You're the most important person in my life. I love you first, okay?"

"I love you first too, Mom." She sighs, when I caress her hair.

Crisis averted, hopefully.

After a few seconds, she leans back and looks up at me, her eyebrows pulled together in a frown. "Let's ask him to the zoo with us. Then we'll know if he's going to be nice to me."

The zoo? On Sunday? This is turning into a trial by fire for the both of us. I hadn't planned on introducing them this quickly!

"Let me think about it, okay?"

"Okay…" Gracie finishes her juice and puts the empty glass up on the counter. I pick it up and rinse it in the sink.

"Now, time for bed. Or you'll be too tired to get up in time for school."

"Okay, Mom."

I walk Grace back to her bedroom, tucking her in just as I'd already done half an hour previous. Hopefully this time she's going to stay put. Jesus. I can't even imagine what would have happened if I'd put my earlier plan into action, started taking the conversation into a more intimate direction, only for Gracie to walk in right then! How would I even explain that! We haven't even had the sex conversation yet!

"Nighty-night, sweet pea," I tell her, while giving her a kiss on her forehead.

"Goodnight, Mom."

* Daniel *

When Kate cut the call so abruptly, my mind started to feed me all kinds of horror scenarios. Her kid overheard our conversation, that much was obvious. And Kate went into damage control mode immediately.

Her daughter is her world. And I'm an intruder.

She wasn't ready for us to meet, and it follows that she wasn't ready to tell her daughter she was dating anyone. Maybe she never planned to; maybe she always planned to keep us separate?

There's that honesty, or lack thereof, rearing its ugly head. Maybe I should have been more direct about things, rather than taking a backseat and avoiding the topic for the most part? Should I have shown more of an interest in her home situation and been clearer about my own intentions?

Instead, Grace overheard us talk, and Kate evidently freaked out about it.

She doesn't think I have what it takes. That's why despite talking about her all the time, she never even showed me her picture.

I thought it might have been too soon for her, but what if that wasn't the real reason?

Honestly, can I blame her? Do I know what a healthy father figure even looks like? All I've ever known is the perfect example of the opposite. Cold, dismissive, authoritarian, even abusive at times... I can tell myself all I want that I would never repeat my father's mistakes, but how would I know? I've never even been in a relationship before this!

The phone ringer interrupts my intrusive thoughts, and while my first instinct is to avoid it, I take a deep breath and do the right thing.

"Hey! Everything okay at your end?" I ask.

Kate chuckles nervously. "So, Grace snuck out of bed and walked in on our conversation."

Yeah, that much I put together on my own. What do I say, though? I'm still trying to think of something, when Kate sighs on the other end of the line, and starts talking again.

"You know how kids can be brutally honest sometimes?" she asks.

"Right."

"She said something which made me think…" Kate's voice trembles as she speaks.

She takes another deep breath, while I wait for her to carry on. Here it comes. Inevitable rejection. I close my eyes and tense up, almost bracing myself for impact. It would be justified, knowing everything I know about myself.

"Well, it boils down to: she wants to meet you. To find out if you're going to be nice to her, in her own words." Kate chuckles briefly. "And although she's much too young to know about relationships yet, she has a point. This thing between us can only work out if the two of you get along as well."

I open my eyes again. That's all? All the panic I felt just now about Kate wanting to keep me away from her daughter, and now… Kids do tend to like me, most of the time.

"And so, I was wondering if—" There's some nervous rustling on the other end of the line.

"She's absolutely correct," I hear myself say. "Smart kid."

"That she is. Very smart." Kate's voice softens a little. "Do you want to go to the zoo with us? I already promised to take her on Sunday, so…"

That sounds perfect. Too good to be true. "I'd love to."

"Whew, okay. I was worried for a second there."

"Worried, why?" I ask.

"Ah, well… Things get so complicated once you bring children into it. There's so much more at stake, all of a sudden."

I let her words sink in for a moment. And I remember everything I've been mulling over about father figures, and everything else.

"I'd never hurt her. Or you," I say. I'd do everything in my power not to.

She exhales sharply, or sighs; I can't tell. "Thanks, Daniel."

It's as if I can hear her smile at me while she says that. And as soon as I do, I can see her smile in my mind's eye as well. And for a moment, everything feels better and brighter again.

"Let's still meet up on Saturday as well," I suggest. If she is going to introduce me to her daughter on Sunday, I still want to tell her my history beforehand. Give her all the information, and let her decide how to proceed from there.

CHAPTER ELEVEN

* Kate *

This week passes even quicker than the last. It's all Daniel. Or rather, my nightly conversations with him. How easy life suddenly seems when you have someone to confide in every day. I never knew how badly I needed just that.

We're growing more comfortable with each other, making me feel that maybe Sunday's zoo plan with Grace isn't too rushed after all.

Kids can be so wise. *Of course* there's no point in carrying on this relationship unless Grace fits into the picture too. *Of course* it would make sense to make sure early on, before I find myself too attached and heartbroken, should it not work out.

Then again, I'm already attached. I would already be heartbroken. But if this is any indicator of how fast I'm falling for Daniel, waiting any longer could potentially make things much, much worse for everyone involved.

And so, I'm staying positive and enjoying the high of being freshly in love. Who knows, maybe this is it? Maybe he turns out to be the one? Grace certainly deserves to have a father figure in her life, just like every other little girl does. Someone to play with her, support her, and make her feel safe. Just like Daniel has made *me* feel safe when he put his arms around me last weekend, or when he called me up every day this week, and sent me a sweet message every morning to start my day with.

We had a somewhat rocky start due to his reluctance to pick up the phone after our televised first date, but I understood his reasons. And anyway, I haven't noticed any red flags since. Maybe Claire could tell all along; he really is a great guy and I just needed to give him a chance.

And so I find myself walking with a spring in my step on the way to our third official date: grabbing a cup of coffee in a quaint little cafe smack bang in the middle of Teddington High Street. We'll be spending a few hours together while Grace has a playdate over at Lucy's house nearby.

It's a quirky place, which I came across completely by chance on social media. Apparently, the only thing better than the coffee are the cinnamon rolls. I'm keen to give those a shot if Daniel is willing to share one. I'm a romantic like that.

He's already there when I arrive, sitting in one of the armchairs towards the back of the cafe, as far away from the counter as can be. There's plenty of footfall of people coming in and out for their takeaway coffee, so I'm glad he reserved a quiet spot for us already.

"Hey, Daniel!" I greet him with a bright smile. He gets up to help me into my chair, but I go in straight for a hug, and don't let go for a blissful few seconds, letting my lungs fill completely with his scent. It's dizzying, the effect he has on me. "I'm so glad we decided to meet today after all."

He squeezes me tightly, and I feel even more at home. "Me too. You look beautiful as ever, by the way."

I look down at my comparatively simple outfit of fitted jeans and cute summer top and smile again. I'd had some trouble striking a balance between wanting to look nice for him, and not sticking out like crazy in what is in essence a very casual coffee joint. It's the heels. Heels make everything work, I decide.

"You look pretty sharp as well, I have to say. I like your shirt," I tell him. The red and black is giving him that lumberjack vibe I seem to be developing a fetish for. Part of it is the beard, as well. God, I love a man with a beard.

He doesn't say anything while helping me into my seat. Guess he's better at giving compliments than accepting them. That's fine. We can work on that.

"Shall I order for us?" he asks.

I lean back to study the menu on the wall behind the counter. Ah, who am I kidding. I already know what I want.

"A medium cappuccino for me, please. No frills," I say. Maybe I'll try the cinnamon roll in a little while, in case we get another round of coffee. But most of all I want to just sit here and look at him. Although we spoke every day after work, I've really missed him. Totally forgot what that's like: being so smitten with someone you miss them every second you're apart.

He comes back a few minutes later with a tray containing two identical looking cups, and I'm still smiling. And feeling high and overconfident and stupid.

"This is going to sound a little dumb. But I kind of missed you all week," I say, watching him put our drinks down on the table.

His shifting expression is everything. The little smile playing on his lips; the way he's averting his gaze while sitting down opposite me. God, it's adorable. Yep, we're definitely going to have to work on his ability to take a compliment. And I'm going to enjoy every second of it.

"Not dumb. I feel the same way." He looks me directly in the eye as he speaks. It sends a shiver down my spine. *Where have you been all my life?*

My turn to awkwardly avert my gaze. I tear open one of the sugar sachets, spilling half of the contents into the saucer rather than the cup, but I don't even care.

"So, they've started showing teasers for the show already," he remarks.

That comment turns my nerves into anxiety. I so wish we were just a regular couple, without that weird start.

"Yeah. Claire told me that the first episode is going to air soon."

He nods. "Weird, huh? Do you think people will recognize us, you know, after?"

I make a face and shudder. "Ugh, I hope not! I want to be able to keep doing this... Meet up together, without worrying who's around or listening in! In fact, I don't think I'm even going to watch any of it myself. It's too... Ugh!" I shake myself to make my point.

He observes me with his head tilted slightly to the right.

"Why; are you?" I ask.

"Am I, what?"

"Are you going to watch our episode? Or any of the rest of it?"

He pauses for a moment, staring down at his cup. As if my question surprises him. Or he simply hasn't thought about it so far.

"Honestly, I have no idea," he says. "Haven't thought about it yet."

Okay, *but?*

"So, this actually leads me to something I wanted

to tell you about."

He runs his fingertip past the rim of the saucer a few times, almost compulsively so. He's nervous. My heart surges in response. What could he possibly be wanting to tell me, which is making him so anxicus? Aren't we past that kind of thing yet? Can't we keep this date nice and light and fun for a change?

"Okay…"

"I think I mentioned it during the shoot, though not in too much detail…"

"What is it?" I ask. It kind of shocks me how fragile my voice sounds. All the while, I'm wracking my brain for what he means. He told me a bunch of things during that first date.

"About my past… About my weight issues." He looks up, but only briefly. It kills me how tense his expression has become.

"Right, you did mention that." Should I lean over and reach out? Surely we're at a stage now where that's acceptable, if not expected. I wish I could make this feeling go away. This awkwardness that's making the air between us feel heavy and thick. If I could run, I would.

"They're going to show pictures. On the show." He clears his throat.

My mind is still racing. So… he's afraid of me seeing the pictures? Why? That's all in the past, and this is now.

"You think I'm going to judge you?" I ask. I hope it doesn't sound like I'm accusing him, because that's not my intention. I'm just trying to figure out what he's really nervous about. Anything, to defuse this weirdness.

He chuckles awkwardly. "I wouldn't blame you."

Okay, so *he's* judging *himself.* I lean forward and indeed follow through on my earlier impulse. I take his hand. He reciprocates and threads his fingers through mine, allowing me to breathe a little easier.

"I won't. I think I said something to this effect even then. We all have something in our past. It wouldn't be right to judge other people for their struggles, whatever they are."

"But, you don't *know*…" he mumbles. "You're all kinds of amazing. And I'm… I was…"

My heart is still racing and my throat is about to close up. I need for this tension to end before I lose my nerve completely.

"Okay, let's put the issue to bed right now," I tell him. "Show me a picture."

He briefly looks into my eyes. This is important to him. I can see it. I just hope I'm able to give him what he needs. To reassure him. To accept where he came from, what made him into the man he is today.

"Okay." He gets his phone out of his pocket and starts scrolling.

I keep quiet and continue to hold his hand, which

is getting clammier by the second. The gravity of the moment isn't lost on me, so I try my best to remain level-headed. Claire told me too much about him when she was still trying to convince me to come on the show. Things that weren't hers to share. Luckily, she didn't tell me this. At least I don't have to feign ignorance about something that evidently still affects him so deeply today. Though a part of me wishes I could have had a head's up to curate my reaction.

I take a deep breath and hold it for a few seconds.

All I have to do is to just accept him. I can do that. I know I can. No matter what he's about to show me, it won't change how I feel about him now. The past is the past. My past bullshit doesn't affect who I am today, so why should his?

He's still looking for that picture with his free hand. His thumb is trembling a little, and then he pauses. His other hand twitches a little, as if he's about to withdraw from my touch, but he doesn't. And I don't either, no matter how badly I want to shut down and hide. I keep trying to hold my breath.

He finally lays the phone down between us, sliding it across. "That was four years ago."

I lean forward and look at the picture. And I'm shocked. Not so much by his physical appearance, because if the difference wasn't significant, he wouldn't have made this big a deal about it. But I wasn't ready to see his face, the coldness in his eyes.

It's like an entirely different person is looking into the camera lens. Someone I don't know at all.

I glance up at him and find him studying my face already.

"Told you," he whispers.

I'm shaken.

"You said so yourself, you've come a long way." I force a smile, but it feels so fake, it probably looks even worse than it feels.

"Yes." He doesn't smile back at me. In fact, the look in his eyes is so guarded, I barely know what to do. And so I keep clinging onto his hand, unsure of what to say to make things better. I don't have much of a poker face. He saw how much his picture stunned me. I fucked up. This is exactly why I should have run!

"I'm not judging you. Who the hell am I to judge anyone?" I wonder aloud.

He takes a deep breath and looks away. "Your expression tells me otherwise."

My mind is spinning. I promised him honesty. And I've been trying to keep that promise ever since, no matter how hard it is. But I do have an explanation. I just hope he's willing to hear it. The only catch is, it requires me to admit something I've been trying so hard to keep under wraps.

"This picture is hard to look at, because…" I zoom into it, noticing how my index finger and thumb tremble as I do so. Then, I turn the phone around to show him. "Because I barely recognize you. All I see in your eyes here—" I point at the photo again, "—is sadness. And that doesn't match the man who's sitting in front of me right now." *The man I've started developing some pretty deep feelings for.*

"And yet… I am the same person," he says.

"You mentioned you had to work through some mental health issues in your past. I didn't expect to be able to see those challenges written on your face like that. That's what's gotten to me. Not your weight. I don't care about that."

My own statement surprises me a little. Because I realize that I really don't care about that. It *really* is the look in his eyes I can't stand to see.

"Written on my face, as well as everywhere else."

"Honestly, I might have quite a few photos like this one, hidden away in an old shoebox somewhere," I mumble. Ever since say, age fifteen or so? They're all quite similar. Even when I'm smiling for the camera, they don't fool me one bit. That's why I refuse to look at pictures of myself from back in the day.

"Not quite like this one, though?" I know what he means, and I'm not taking the bait.

I take a deep breath and fight like hell to maintain eye contact with him. Despite the worry and the awkwardness and shame I see in him now. He's right, of course. Deep down, he still is that same person. Whether I like it or not.

"I recognize the look in your eyes, because it's all too familiar to me. I've been there. No matter how hard I try to forget," I whisper.

During our first date he made a comment about what he'd say to his past self. Very similar to what I'd tell my own past self, if I could. So, this was Daniel four years ago. Shit. I'm in awe of how far he's come. It's been a little longer for me, despite having Grace to keep me on track. And any combination of words I can think of to tell him how much I admire him right now would just come across as patronizing.

"Daniel, thanks for showing me. For letting me understand you better." Ugh, that still sounds cringey. "This doesn't change my feelings about us." My feelings. Which I haven't dared to define yet.

He picks up his phone, locks the screen, and puts it away in silence.

"Now it's all out in the open. No more surprises," he mumbles.

I bite my bottom lip as I carry on staring at him. Do I dare? Do I dare say what's on the tip of my tongue right now? Will he run for the hills? Then again, *honesty*. Honesty is the thing that matters most to me in a relationship, and also the most difficult thing for me to practice myself. Because every time I've tried to be honest in the past, I've had it thrown back in my face.

Ugh. Why do relationships have to be so hard!

"I…" I take a deep breath and squeeze down on his hand, desperate for reassurance that he's listening. His thumb briefly caresses past my knuckles, giving me that little push I need.

"I think I love you," I whisper.

CHAPTER TWELVE

*** Daniel ***

We end up spending three hours at the weird little coffee shop Kate picked out for our third date, and it still feels short. I'm still on cloud nine when we say our goodbyes.

She told me she loves me.

After being stunned into silence for what had to have been the longest twenty seconds in the history of time itself, I told her that I love her too. The most difficult combination of words in the English language. Nothing could prepare me for how that felt. And our exchange happened only moments after I was certain I'd put her off by confronting her with my past self. No matter how hard she tried to convince me that her feelings hadn't changed after seeing my old picture, I didn't believe her until I heard those words come out of her mouth. She *loves* me.

Kate continues to surprise me. And after we sat in silence together, just holding hands and staring into each other's eyes following our confessions, the other things she'd said started to sink in. That we actually do all have things in our past we'd rather forget about. We all have had to live through our share of challenges. Even someone as outwardly perfect as she is. Who would have thought?

I felt like asking her about what it was for her, but her reluctance to discuss the matter was clear as day. And then she told me she loved me, and nothing else seemed to matter anymore.

Maybe the impulsive decision to sign up for a stupid reality show has turned out to be the best thing to ever happen to me. Maybe now is the moment in time I'll be able to look back on later to say: this is when it all changed for me. This is when my luck turned. When my life truly began.

My life with her, hopefully.

When I walk her to her car and give her a big hug and a kiss, the last thing I want is to let go. We make out in the parking lot for a minute. Just long enough for it to be inappropriate should anyone see, but not long enough to satisfy either of us.

She's amazing. The perfect woman. And she loves *me*. How the fuck did that happen?

After two-and-a-half dates and daily phone calls in between? I've done nothing special, just been myself and showed some vulnerability. Like Owen advised. Maybe he was onto something, crazy as it seems. Then again, even a broken clock is right twice a day.

And the best part of today is getting to see Kate again tomorrow. And meet Grace on top of it. Now

I'm really going to have to do my best to impress her little girl, because she clearly has veto power.

Another, lesser man would feel threatened by the prospect of that. Maybe even have his ego hurt. But to me, it's beautiful. Because a relationship between a parent and child *should* be like that. They should come first, and everything else, second. Not like how my childhood was, and perhaps even Kate's from the sound of things. I deeply respect her for prioritizing her daughter above everything and everyone else.

I'll gladly come second to Grace, if it means I can be a part of their lives going forward. It would be an honor.

Upon reaching home, I'm greeted by Jack, who in his exuberance decides to jump all over me. I might need to reign that in before introducing him to Kate and especially Grace…

But for now, I let myself enjoy his excitement, as well as that little signature bark of his which sounds halfway like a howl. *Wowowowow!* It's the sweetest thing.

The love I feel when I look at his little face must be just a fraction of what Kate feels for her daughter. That's crazy. To love another person so deeply.

The old me might have found it hard to believe, but now… After learning what it's like to hear those words from another human being… *I love you…* It doesn't feel so far-fetched anymore.

I make my way through the hallway and into the lounge, where I sit on the couch, allowing Jack to hop into my lap and lick my nose. It's the best.

Kate and Grace are going to love him too, and he will love them right back; I just know it. It would be impossible not to.

Maybe, if tomorrow goes well, I'll propose we all meet at the dog park next? That could be fun.

Just as Jack starts to settle down, my phone buzzes in my pocket. I take it out to check the notification. It's from Kate.

'Missing you already…x'

Me too, Kate. Me too.

* Kate *

We're late leaving the house as usual. So we'll be late meeting Daniel at the zoo as well.

Grace is still putting on her shoes, and I can't find my keys. It's the nerves. So much is riding on today! But I'm not just terrified, I'm excited as well. Because I can't wait to see him again. I can't wait to spend the day, walking hand-in-hand through the zoo, having eyes for him more than all the exhibits Grace is so keen to visit.

This was a good decision, wasn't it? And he certainly didn't hesitate to accept, meaning he's ready for this next step too?

God, I hope so, because I don't know how I'd cut him out of my life now. Ridiculous, considering we only met a few weeks ago. Still, through our daily chats and especially yesterday's coffee date, it's like I've known him forever. That's the level of comfort I feel when I look him in the eyes.

The warmth. The excitement. Even the attraction between us is off the charts.

We kissed briefly after he walked me to my car yesterday, which made me ache for so much more. I had a hard time letting go. That was also a large reason I stayed in bed a little too long this morning. I couldn't tear myself away from all the beautiful dreams my subconscious had served up for me. Of Daniel and I. Our hands all over each other, as well as our mouths…

Maybe tonight we'll get a chance to explore each other in private a little? If all goes well, I plan to ask him to come back with us for dinner, and then… Once Grace goes to bed, who knows what might happen?

But I'm getting ahead of myself as usual. We still have a whole day of family friendly fun to look forward to first. If only we can get organized and get to the station already!

"Gracie, we're getting late for the train!" I call out while holding her jacket up in her direction.

"I know, Mom!" she says while carefully putting

Ed the octopus down next to the shoe rack in the hallway. "I'm sorry, you can't come with us. See you later, Ed!"

* Daniel *

Today has gone so much better than expected. Grace is even more of an angel than Kate said. And we got along famously, just as I'd hoped.

A funny thing started to happen, right from our first meeting. The more I kept observing Grace, the more of Kate I recognized in her. It was magical, seeing all the best parts of a person reflected in a little version of them.

Now I'm not just in love with Kate, I'm in love with Grace too. In the best possible way. I would give anything—I'd literally die for this child if I had to. And so when I caught her eyeing the vast array of stuffed toys at the gift shop, I couldn't help myself and bought her whatever she wanted. I didn't even think to ask Kate if it was okay. Because there was no way I could say no to those big pleading eyes.

And even now, she's hugging the ridiculously large stuffed crocodile against herself and I'm overflowing with emotions. It's a beautiful sight to see her so happy.

"That was a bit extra," Kate teases, when she catches me watching her.

"How the hell was I supposed to refuse?" I ask. "Just look at her!"

She laughs. "That's the trick to parenting. Or they'll turn into spoiled little brats."

"That's fine. You can handle the discipline side of things. I don't think I have it in me."

Kate is still laughing when I turn towards her and just for a second, cup her beautiful face and kiss her on the lips. Just like that. Like it's the most normal thing in the world. Grace is walking ahead of us and not paying attention anyway, so it seems safe enough.

"Thanks for including me today," I tell her.

She looks up at me, in awe. I wish she'd never stop looking at me like this. It occurs to me that I could never refuse her anything either. So, I'm about to have not one but two women wrapping me around their little finger. No problem. Whatever they want.

"Thanks for being such a good sport," she whispers, before kissing me back.

"It's been my pleasure."

"You're the best, you know that?" she says.

I shake my head. "Both of you are. I'm just along for the ride."

"You've got to learn how to take a compliment." She smiles.

I smile back at her. This is alien. This is bliss.

"I love you," I tell her. It feels lighter this time. Easier. Effortless, like Owen might observe.

"I love you too," she says.

Will I ever tire of hearing those words? Probably not. Because I never once heard them said to me before meeting her. Now, whenever I do, everything feels right in the world.

"You guys! Hurry up, they're about to start feeding the penguins and we'll miss it!" Grace calls out ahead of us, prompting us to start walking again.

I never once let go of Kate's hand for the remainder of the afternoon. Not when we indeed see the penguins being fed. Nor when we visit the reptiles; the primates; the outdoor enclosures where they keep the large cats. I just can't bring myself to stop. And she doesn't make any attempt to either.

Not until it's time to make our way back home, or rather, to Kate and Gracie's home, anyway, when I gladly volunteer to drive the three of us. Hopefully Jack will be okay to stay by himself a little while longer after the long walk I took him on this morning and the dog sitter who I arranged for to take him out in the afternoon.

It tickles me to be included for family dinner with them, and to be able to see more of their lives up close. Selfishly, I want to absorb everything there is to know about these two. I want…

I want to be a part of their lives going forward.

It's a strange realization, one which fills me with warmth and excitement as well as a healthy dose of trepidation. Do I have what it takes to take care of them? God, I hope so. Or else I'll make it my mission in life to learn. Because every time either one of them smiles at me, it gives me life all over again. I just can't get enough.

And that high follows me. Through the somewhat challenging traffic along the way. Up to the modern-looking apartment where they live. In every little exchange and every question Grace shoots my way about this and that; what animal was my favorite and why; as well as an in depth interrogation about Jack's favorite snacks and toys…

I don't even recognize it at first, and then, it strikes me. This is what it's like to be accepted. To belong. And when Kate reaches over and puts her hand on my knee, that turns things up to eleven. Because that isn't just warm and fuzzy, that's searingly hot as well.

Is it always like this, love? No wonder people do stupid things for it. It's hard to think straight, with so much chaos going on inside.

We walk up to the door of their apartment. I can't help but steal glances at the two of them. How alike they are. Not just in terms of looks, but mannerisms as well.

"Do make yourself at home," Kate tells me, while she leads the way into the spacious and beautifully decorated living area. Stylish. Like the rest of her. "I'll get started on dinner."

"Can I help in any way?" I ask.

She shakes her head and smiles. "Not tonight. This one's on me."

Grace grabs my hand and tugs at it.

"Wanna go see my room?" she asks.

I can't help but grin at her enthusiasm. "Of course, I want the full tour!"

She smiles back at me and I fall a little deeper. How am I allowed to be here right now? How did this happen?

"Okay, follow me!" Grace announces, before marching down the narrow hallway towards a door with origami flowers stuck to it, as well as a nameplate she must have colored in herself. It's adorable, just like her.

The room is pretty and airy, and has an impressive collection of stuffed toys lined up on multiple wall shelves. The crocodile she insisted on getting at the zoo is by far the biggest toy she's got, though. She places it carefully on her bed, along with the bright blue octopus she'd picked up as soon as we entered the house.

"So, this is Ed," Grace says, holding up the octopus. Then she places her hand on top of the crocodile's head. "I don't have a name for this new one yet… I'll have to think about it."

I can't help but smile. "It's a big decision, you'd better take your time."

"I know!"

"How about the others?" I point at the rest of the collection, looking down on us like a very cute, very colorful audience.

"Okay, so this one's Kevin, and Jane, and this little one is called Fluffy…" she says, pointing out a few of them from left to right.

"Right. I can see where Fluffy gets his name from. May I see?" I ask.

She thinks for a moment, then smiles. "Sure, I guess that would be okay."

Grace stands up on her tippy toes and slowly takes the extremely shaggy purple monster toy off the shelf, careful not to disturb any of the others. Then she hugs it against herself for a second.

"Fluffy has a secret, you know…" she says mysteriously.

"Oh does he? I won't tell, I promise."

She presses her lips together tightly, then solemnly hands me the toy. "Turn him over," she instructs.

I do as she says and see that there's something tucked inside a partially open seam at the back of it.

"What's this?" I ask.

"Promise you won't tell Mom."

I place my index finger on my lips in silence.

"Here." She reaches for the toy, then removes the piece of paper that was hidden inside the toy and holds it up in front of me. "I found this in Mom's old things. That's my dad."

I smile and nod politely. This photograph is obviously very precious to her. Kate mentioned that Grace's father isn't in the picture anymore, so perhaps this is all she has to remind her of him?

I lean forward to look at it, more to humor her than anything.

"That's a very nice picture of the two of them…" my voice trails off towards the end, because that's when I actually stop to study it properly.

Kate is Kate, obviously. A few years younger, but every bit the woman I've fallen in love with. And the man with his arm possessively hooked around her. . I expected some nameless stranger. Someone I've never seen before.

It's not.

It's a face I know all too well. A face I haven't thought about in decades. Blake-fucking-Callahan, who grew up two streets over from me and never missed a chance to make a bad day worse.

It's been a long time. Over twenty years. And yet…

"Very nice," I tell Grace, while handing the photograph back to her. My heart is racing, my hands clammy. *This* is Grace's dad? It would have been better not to know.

"So, now, this one is Dumbo. Because he's an elephant, you see?" Grace chatters on while pointing up at the shelf.

I take a deep breath. And another. All the while trying to keep the conversation going. My mind, however, is a million miles away. Or rather, about twenty-two years away.

Obviously I knew Kate had a past with another guy, and that's fine. Did it have to be *this* particular guy, though? This bottom-of-the-barrel scum of humanity? My childhood nemesis. The literal opposite of everything I am?

As much as it pains me, it makes me see her differently. Not Grace, but Kate. It makes me question things all over again.

I carry on trying to breathe and smile and play it cool. Trying to think. There must be a justification. Some kind of missing detail to make all this make sense. There's a reason they didn't work out as a couple. This doesn't need to change anything. This doesn't—

"Dinner's ready!" Kate's voice interrupts my racing thoughts.

"Coming, Mom!" Grace calls out. "Are you also coming? Mom doesn't like to wait with dinner."

"Uh-huh. Yeah." I gesture at her to lead the way and follow behind her, watching her skip towards the fully laid out dining table, blissfully unaware of how her little secret affected me.

I just have to get through this meal. At some

point, it'll be bedtime for Grace, and I'll get the chance to ask Kate…

Or maybe I should just keep my trap shut? Maybe I should let this topic lie in the past where it belongs?

I can't, though. I can't just ignore this. Because I can't stop myself from jumping to conclusions, all of which are bad.

Deep breaths. *It's okay. Everything will be okay. She didn't know how terrible he was, and once she found out, she dumped his ass. Breathe!*

"I hope you like pasta," Kate says, while almost apologetically pointing at the dish in the center of the table.

I nod. "My favorite."

"Mine too!" Grace chirps. She makes me smile despite myself.

Yes, there has to be an explanation. I'm getting carried away over nothing.

CHAPTER THIRTEEN

*** Kate ***

I wake up early, pondering over the events from last night. The day went so very well, and then… something weird happened after I put Grace to bed. Our conversation no longer flowed. I tried to steer him away from talking about Blake, but he wasn't having it. Not that we had a fight or anything, but the vibe was off.

I'd wanted to snuggle on the sofa with him, maybe watch a movie, or share a glass of wine and see where things would lead… Just have a pleasant, perhaps even intimate evening together. But nothing felt right. So we kept on sitting at the dining table, forcing a conversation that wasn't flowing.

I guess I should have listened to my instincts. It *was* too early to bring Grace into it.

He might have had the best of intentions, but the reality of being confronted with another man's child turned out to be too much, too soon. That's why he kept prying; kept asking me about my relationship with Blake; kept picking at scars that I thought had healed a long time ago.

It was uncomfortable, bordering on inappropriate. And if I wasn't already so in love with him, I would have put my foot down and told him off more than once.

I'm no longer as hung up on everything that happened with Blake as I once was. All that stuff is firmly in the past where it belongs. But I'm not ready to lay the whole painful truth out there in front of Daniel. We're not there yet. I don't know what has to happen for that to change, but right now it feels wrong to me.

He's jealous.

That's what it is. He's jealous of a man from my past, which makes perfect sense when you think about it. Maybe Daniel is the one judging *me* now. For having a child with another man and ending up single right after.

Ugh.

It's too painful a thought. And I hope I'm wrong about it. But I can't stop coming back to this conclusion. It's all I could think about until I finally drifted off to sleep last night. Even my dreams told me as much.

This is his first relationship, and maybe deep down he had hoped that it would be the same for his eventual partner? And here I am, with living proof of a history with someone else.

Could it be that simple?

And if it is, can we get past it? I hope so, because we've been nothing short of amazing together otherwise. He's patient, caring, attentive. And so very good with Grace as well, at least during our time at the zoo.

That's why the weirdness of last night came as a shock to me. Was I wrong about him after all? Had I missed an important warning sign leading up to this point? We've had a few heavy conversations, but always managed to turn things around. Why couldn't he respect my desire not to discuss my past with Blake? Why keep at it, unless there was something deeper, like jealousy, at work?

Is he exactly like the others, unable to accept me for who I really am, past history and all?

When my alarm finally goes off, I take a deep breath and force myself up. I'm exhausted. More so than I was at my worst recently, shortly before our first date. My limbs feel heavy and my head is dull. And it's Monday morning. The beginning of what is promising to be a trying week, thanks to Evelyn and her never-ending nonsense.

I drag myself out of bed, and quickly pop into Gracie's room to wake her too. There she is, a little blonde haired angel, sleep-hugging her brand new stuffed crocodile against herself. Daniel bought that for her, simply because. It was cute and heartwarming at the time. And now it's going to remind me of him, and all my doubts about us, every time I see the bloody thing.

Luckily Grace remains blissfully unaware of everything, and I hope to keep it that way.

"Gracie, time to get up!" I tell her while walking up to her bedside, putting on a bright smile just for her.

She stirs, but doesn't open her eyes just yet. "Wakey-wakey!"

I lean across and kiss her on her forehead. That's when she finally looks up.

"Mom! Do I have to?" She stretches and hides her face in her new toy.

"Don't you want to tell all your friends about your day at the zoo yesterday?"

Her eyes widen and she grins at me. "Oh yes! They're going to be so, so jealous!"

I ruffle her hair and smile back at her again. Even though I'm still torn inside.

It was a pretty good day, despite what followed.

Then again, maybe I'm making a mountain out of a molehill. *You'll see, he'll send you a good morning message as usual, and all will be well! You can talk it out later like grownups and nothing needs to change.*

I sigh deeply and watch as Grace gets out of bed and straightens her sheets just like I taught her to. She's such a good girl. I wonder where she gets it from sometimes. At her age, I certainly wasn't making my own bed. I still don't on some days, today being one of them.

Our usual morning routine takes an hour and a half. Luckily Grace is self-sufficient, and gets herself ready for school without much of a fuss. How quickly she has grown already.

And that's for the best, because I keep losing time staring at my phone. Waiting, hoping, wishing for all my worries to be unfounded.

And no message comes at the usual time. Just silence.

And those same nagging thoughts that plagued me all night keep bubbling back up every so often. What if we can't get past it? What if he doesn't reach out? What will I tell Grace? How will I soothe the gaping hole that's suddenly opened up in my chest?

You want something done, you've got to do it yourself, my inner voice tries to tell me. And plus, I do always try to advise Grace to give people the benefit of the doubt at least once. Allow them to explain themselves when they've done something to hurt us.

If *he* doesn't message or call today, then I will reach out first. One more chance. Just this once.

* Daniel *

The fantasy is broken. No matter how high the peaks of our admittedly short relationship so far, the hole I find myself in come Monday morning seems too deep to be able to climb out of. Nothing is as it seemed.

I still send her a quick good morning message, more out of habit than anything else. It's a bit short and hours later than normal, but that's the best I could manage. Because I don't know what's next now. I don't know how this is supposed to work.

Blake is little Grace's dad. Of course he is. Because literally what could be worse than for the person I hate most in the world to be Kate's ex? Nothing. There could be nothing worse.

Because he's everything I am not. Cocky, handsome, star player of the rugby club near where we grew up, and a total fucking psychopath. And if *that's* the sort of guy she's attracted to, then what the hell are we playing at here?

To think she actually told me on Saturday that my past issues didn't change anything for her. That she loved me anyway. What a joke. So I did see what I thought I saw when she looked at my old picture. It wasn't about the supposed sadness in my eyes. That was bullshit. It was and always will be about looks and expectations.

That picture was a stark reminder of just how much she's settling by being with me.

Because I'm not the one. I don't measure up. Never did and never will.

There are winners and losers in this world, and

I've been reminded of my place once again.

My phone lights up with another call I can't bring myself to answer. So I just stare at it, almost catatonically, while waiting for the ringer to stop.

How many times will she try, before giving up? Three, four times? Maybe I should man up and tell her it's over. That I will not be someone's second choice. Especially not second choice to Blake-fucking-Callahan.

Because you're such a fucking prize you deserve to be first choice, right?

Fuck.

I should have just followed my instinct, whenever it spoke up to feed me doubts about what was unfolding between us. I shouldn't have fallen for it. Guys like me don't get a break. And they certainly don't get the girl.

I turn on the TV in an effort to drown out the noise in my head. A familiar logo fills the screen, just as some cheesy theme music starts to play.

Sealed with a Kiss, coming this month! Really, universe?!

I switch it off and fling the remote across the room in disgust. It splits apart and the batteries scatter across the floor. What a perfect visual for how I feel. Broken apart, with my guts spilled out.

Kate is everything. Beautiful, smart, independent, and an amazing mother. Who am I to think I could have a chance with her? That she could pick me?

And maybe she truly believed it when she said she values honesty and loyalty in a relationship, over everything else. She might want to think that, but people often don't know what they really believe. Until they come face-to-face with the starkness of reality.

The fact that she wouldn't tell me about what happened with Blake really told me everything I needed to know. This thing we shared is her backup plan. It's a consolation prize, because the one she really wanted didn't stick around. That she has her own wounds from her past, which tell her to settle for me. A nice enough guy, who would be devoted to her and her little girl because he'd know the both of them are way out of his league.

Who am I, anyway? I'm not the hero of this story, I'm the supporting character, the comic relief. I just never realized it until now. That's why the first two blind dates they set me up on didn't work out. Those other women could see it from a mile away. I'm no prize. I'm nothing.

And yet, for all my hard-fought self-awareness, I can't bring myself to swallow my pride and accept my place in the hierarchy.

I can't.

Because it hurts too damn much.

Because I wanted it to be me. For once, I wanted to be someone. Grace would always come first for

Kate, I was happy to accept that. But not this. I'm unwilling to be third in line, with Blake still reminding me of his dominance even in his absence. I couldn't stand up to him when I was twelve, and I still can't, even indirectly.

My phone lights up again, but this time with a message rather than a call.

'Can we talk, please?' Kate writes. 'I'm worried about you.'

Talk. That would be the right thing—the mature thing—to do. And yet, I can't. Not right now. It was hard enough to get out of bed to feed Jack this morning. It took me hours more just to leave the house to take him for a short walk around the block.

But all this while, my throat and chest have been so tight, I wouldn't know how to get a word out. I'm blocked. Frozen.

'I'm sorry. It's been a busy day today,' I answer. 'Don't worry, I'm fine.'

Send.

I'm not fine. I will be, though. Maybe. Eventually. But it isn't something she can help me with, so what's the point in talking about it?

Fuck. I thought I was over this.

I might look different now than in the picture I showed her on Saturday, but the 'sadness' that supposedly shocked her so much remained in me all along. It was just hidden away, lying in wait. And today it's all come clawing back out. To drag me back down to where I started. And all the rationalizing in the world can't get me past that. Because everything I try to tell myself to make this okay sounds like a lie.

Despite what Owen said, I wasn't ready. I was never prepared for this. I should have known better. Hell, *he* should have known better too, considering he's such a bloody expert. After all the questionnaires he made me fill out and all the conversations we had.

I had no clue how much this could hurt. Love should come with a warning label attached. *May end in the complete and total destruction of the self.*

It's not even Kate's fault. I can't blame her for any of this. My decisions led me up to this point. My fault for flying too high and getting burned.

My fault. I turn over to stare at the other wall. Jack curls up behind me; I can feel his warmth pressed up against the small of my back. That's what I try to focus on. That's what still allows me to keep breathing. If not for him, I don't know where I'd be right now.

CHAPTER FOURTEEN

*** Kate ***

Monday sucked, Tuesday is worse, and Wednesday takes things to whole new depths. After calling and messaging Daniel on Monday evening, and getting that puzzling and rather cold response back, I decided to pull back and let him make the next move. I'm hurt, but I'm not about to chase someone who can't deal with my past.

Been there and done that before. I refuse to do it again.

The work Evelyn dumped on me yesterday is still sitting there on my desk, untouched. It's only a matter of time until she comes and gives me a hard time about it. And I couldn't give a fuck anymore. I'm good at my job. I always get everything done on time, and to a high standard.

Certainly better than most of my colleagues, who'd rather gossip around the water cooler.

The fact that she keeps adding to my workload isn't just unfair, it's unconscionable. And I frankly don't have the spoons to deal with it. Not right now. Not anymore.

"Kate, didn't I make it clear how important this was? What's your excuse this time?" Evelyn's voice is so shrill it actually hurts my ears. The headache that's been lingering all day every day doesn't help either.

And something inside me, which has been festering for much too long, snaps.

"Well, let me tell you all about it, Evelyn," I say, while turning around on my chair to face her head-on. "How about, I'm not doing your job for you anymore? How about that for an excuse? Because if I'm expected to take on your responsibilities on top of my own, I'm being woefully underpaid as well as under appreciated in this place!"

She opens her mouth, then closes it again. All the while, her nostrils are flaring, and her chest is rising and falling in quick succession, that's how angry she is.

But now, as more and more of my colleagues are popping their heads up from their cubicles to look at us, she seems unable to find the words to rebuff me. Because I'm right and she knows it.

"Well, I'll be—" she huffs. "This is unacceptable!"

"I agree! Completely unacceptable. And I'll be forced to take it up with HR if it happens again."

"Do you forget that the MD and I go way back? How do you think that's going to go for you?" Evelyn threatens.

"If there is some preferential treatment going on in this office, then that too is a matter which HR should be made aware of!" I counter.

Somewhere behind Evelyn, someone snickers, and

she flinches.

"This isn't the end of this," she says as she stomps away.

"I certainly hope not," I mumble under my breath.

As soon as she's out of earshot, there's applause. But I feel far from triumphant.

"Good on ya. She's been out of control for a while now," Leslie from two cubicles across tells me.

I nod.

Some of the others from the floor also mumble words of encouragement at me while giving me the thumbs up or walking up to me to pat me on my back. *Where were all of you before this, huh?* I was always the quiet one, always getting everyone's crap dumped on me. No one else ever said a kind word to me then.

But none of that really bothers me. This is just a job. Something you do for money. Money which puts food on the table for Grace, and keeps a roof over our heads. The worst part is, I finally stood up to Evelyn and my first impulse is to message Daniel about it. Because he would have been proud of me, normally. Except, I haven't heard from him since that cryptic message about being 'busy.' *That's* what really hurts. *That's* what really matters.

And that's the one thought which continues to haunt me when I excuse myself to hide in the bathroom. Just in time before silent tears start to flow for the first time since everything fell apart. No way I can let Grace see me like this later. So I do the only thing I can think of to soothe myself. I call Claire. And I cry some more.

With a bit of luck, that'll be enough. And I'll be calm and composed by the time I head over to Gracie's daycare to pick her up. And I won't feel quite so let down and alone. Again.

* Daniel *

My week is a blur. A bottomless chasm of doom.

I'm in between projects, so my business doesn't suffer, but it will soon. And I don't care.

Nothing matters anymore. There's no light at the end.

The only thing dragging me out of bed is Jack, who obviously still expects regular meals and walks. By Wednesday evening, I've run out of dog food, and have resorted to feeding him scraps and leftovers. He's a lot more excited about it than I am. Empty takeout containers litter the floor beside my bed. I can't even bear to look at them, because of what they represent. And every day, the pile grows to add to my shame.

The last time things got close to this extreme… I can't put a date on it, but it's been years.

Years of effort changing bad habits, wiped out overnight. Because seeing Blake's face after so long seemed to turn back time on me. The idea that for Kate, *he* was the one she really wanted… that's what twisted the knife and tore my heart out. Suddenly everything I'd been working towards became meaningless.

I'd forgotten what it was like, not to feel. After the high I'd been riding these last few weeks, the shock of having that ripped out from underneath me made this low even more unbearable.

I've never known the kind of love I felt with Kate. Never known heartache as a result. To be on top of the world, and then to find it wasn't real, at least not from her side… Maybe it's the contrast that makes it worse. Maybe… If I could just find clarity. Some sense of balance!

But I know that I still won't have Kate. Even if I get over myself and accept my place, it will never be how it was. I've lost hope, so I'll be different as a result, even if everything else stays the same.

In a sense, I'm grieving something which I never really had in the first place. Just the illusion of it. And the worst part is, I know what to do to cope now, intellectually. Maintain a routine, eat healthy food, go to the gym, or at least for longer walks to clear my head. I know the steps to take, but I slipped into this dark place and took root there anyway.

Even if I do find the perspective… Even if I do find the strength to climb out.

I will have lost her, still. Everything I ever wanted, over, because of a few stupid choices I made. She'll already never forgive me. How will I ever forgive myself?

How does Blake-fucking-Callahan still have this much power over me? Twenty-two years later? How can he run me into the ground with a look into a camera lens, not even aimed at me? Have I learned nothing? Have I not grown at all?

And Kate's gone. At least my fantasy of her.

Kate…

And sweet little Grace…

What will she think, going forward? Where did that guy go, who came along to the zoo and was never heard from or seen again? I hope she doesn't jump to conclusions. I hope Kate doesn't, either. It's not her fault. It's *my* fault. It's always been, and always will be my fault.

Maybe I can live with that eventually. But I can't let things end like this, open-ended and unresolved. I have to get over myself and actually talk things through.

"What do I do?" I ask.

Jack raises his head and stares at me, wide-eyed and worried.

"What the fuck do I do? And why am I asking a dog for relationship advice?"

I grab my phone. It's dead, because of course it is.

I've barely looked at it since my last message to Kate on Monday.

After plugging it in with trembling fingers, I find myself growing more agitated during the time it takes to switch on. As if my clock is running out, when I've wasted days already. But back then, I hadn't realized it yet. I hadn't figured things out, and so time seemed to stand still. That used to happen to me in the past. I'd spend hours or days, staring at nothing, feeling stuck.

This won't last forever. At least I should figure out how to tell her it wasn't her fault. To make sure she tells Grace too. Those two deserve to find all the happiness in the world, just not with me.

Finally, the phone switches on. And I scroll through my recent call list, staring at Kate's name for much too long. It would be the right thing to do, but I can't.

I swipe down further a bit.

Owen. I literally cannot think of who else to call.

The phone seems to ring endlessly, and I'm about to give up. He's just going to make some snarky remark and I'll want to smash the phone against the wall. And then I won't have a phone anymore either. The only thing keeping Jack and me fed right now.

But then, a click. I close my eyes and try to breathe deeper and slower. It's not working.

"Owen," I start. "I think I need help."

"Yeah. I think so too," he says, in his usual

monotone voice. Can't tell if he's being sarcastic or what. Does it matter anymore if he judges me too? All I know is I need some guidance to get out of this hole I've found myself in. I'll take anything. Even Owen.

"Something happened."

"Tell me."

"You're not busy, I hope?" That sounds disingenuous, even to my own ears, because I mostly don't have it in me to care.

"Not too busy for this," Owen says. "What happened?"

That's… Those words are rather nice to hear, especially from him. I press my lips together, to try and keep all the sadness contained, but I pretty much fail. I've lost all the progress I thought I'd made over the years.

"What happened?" Owen repeats himself.

I open my eyes again, only to find my vision blurred with tears that came out of nowhere. *What a loser. Boys don't cry.* Words I've heard so many times, in so many different voices. One of them, Blake-fucking-Callahan. That guy had a talent for popping up at the worst times of my life.

"It's Kate. I simply froze. It's been days since our last contact. I fucked up and it's not her fault. I want her to know that it's me, not her—I just don't know how to."

"Breathe," Owen says. "First, you just breathe."

I try to. And then I try again.

"Why did you ghost Kate?"

"Because…" Because I'll never be good enough for someone like her. Because it was all a big mistake, a dream that could never be.

"It's okay, Daniel. We'll figure this out."

How will we, when I can't even figure it out properly myself yet?

"Why don't you start at the beginning. What happened when you last saw or spoke to her? The events leading up to that."

I close my eyes again and try to focus. All the memories from that day… They're so vivid still. That's why the loss hurts so deeply.

"On Sunday, I met her little girl. Grace," I tell Owen. Then I tell him about the zoo and the stuffed toy and everything in between. Recounting those memories still makes me feel warm and fuzzy, until I get to the moment that changed everything. The photograph of Kate and Blake together.

"Why does it make a difference who he is? He's out of the picture." That's such an Owen thing to say.

It makes all the difference. Because…!

"We grew up together. He was a menace," I explain.

"People change. He might be different now. Might have been different with Kate. Just as you are different."

Do they? Do people change? I certainly didn't! I'm right back in that same place where I was all those years ago. Helpless to fight him off, even if he's only in my imagination now. A coward.

"I don't feel different."

Owen pauses. The silence between us grows larger and larger, until I can't help but fill it myself.

"It's like I'm reliving those old memories every moment of every day since then."

"But you haven't been reliving them for the past twenty years, have you?" Owen asks.

I shake my head, lost in thought. No…

"In between, you grew into the man you are today. You turned your life around. You left all that stuff behind."

"But I never dealt with it," I say.

"How do you think you ought to deal with it?" Owen says.

"You're the expert. You tell me!"

He's silent again, and I wrack my brain for the answer he seems to want out of me. "I deal with it by… talking to you about it?" I ask.

"Exactly."

That's stupid. It cannot be that simple. I almost feel like hanging up on him, when I take a deep breath and let the urge pass.

"When I saw the picture, I asked Kate about him," I say. That's when it all went to shit.

"What did she say?"

"She played coy. Like she didn't want to talk about it." Because she's not over him. Because *he's* the one she wants, and I'm not.

"Maybe she hasn't dealt with it either," Owen remarks.

I forget to breathe for a moment. Her refusal to discuss Blake wasn't about me, but about her. *Her* history. *Her* pain. Maybe she doesn't want him back. Maybe she simply didn't know what to say?

"She called me on Monday. And then she messaged to ask if we could talk."

Owen remains quiet. Talk. Kate wanted to talk. And I didn't take her up on that. The only woman I've ever loved, and I didn't even talk to her, I just blew her off with some bullshit excuse.

God, it really is my fault. I'm the worst.

"She's not going to forgive me."

"It really hasn't been that long," Owen says.

It hasn't? What day is it, even? Monday feels like an eternity ago.

"Why not pick up the phone and talk to her now?" Owen suggests.

A surge of panic wells up in my chest. *Panic…* That's different. Panic motivates. It makes you run away, or in this case maybe towards something. It's different from the stagnant pit of nothingness I've been stuck in.

Owen has a point. I hate it.

"Do you love her?" he asks.

Well, obviously. Or I wouldn't have cared this much. And at least at the time, she said the words first. *Fuck.* She told me she loved me, and I pulled away from her. I really am the worst.

"Just one more thing…" Owen says.

"Yeah?"

"Actually *listen.* Don't jump to conclusions. A lot of what you're telling me right now is coming from you, not from her. Negative self-talk. All-or-nothing thinking. Catastrophizing. I'm here if you want to get into more depth about all of this, but first, talk to *her.*"

I hate him. Hate that he's right. With his weird dark-rimmed glasses and smug know-it-all face. He might have just saved my skin. The insufferable little—

"Thanks, Owen."

"Any time."

CHAPTER FIFTEEN

* Kate *

It's Thursday night and the doorbell rings, which isn't just unusual this time of day, it's unheard of. I haven't ordered takeout. Nobody ever visits, and certainly not unannounced.

I leave the chain on when I unlock the door, just in case.

"Daniel," I say, upon catching a glimpse of him through the crack, just before my throat nearly closes up.

Before either of us get the chance to say anything else, Grace almost knocks me over, gets up on her tippy toes to undo the chain, and opens the door wide.

"You made my mom sad!" she says accusingly. "Why?"

I bite my lip. I thought I'd done a pretty good job hiding my mood from her. Evidently not.

He leans down and caresses her hair for a second. "I've come to apologize for it, sweetheart."

Grace folds her arms and glares at him. What kind of a mother am I to make her think she needs to protect me? From a man, no less. That's not the kind of message I ever meant to send! I straighten my back to look more confident, but all I want to do is curl up and hide. Or run. Running would be good right now.

"Grace, I think it's best if Daniel and I spoke alone." I try to sound firm, yet calm. And I fail.

She grabs my hand, clinging to it as hard as she can. "No! I'm not going!"

Sweet, infuriating girl, why won't you listen when it matters most? Though, I don't want to talk to him. Talking is the last thing I want. A part of me is grateful she's acting as my buffer. That's even worse. Hiding behind my own child.

"May I come in?" Daniel asks her. The fact that he's letting her call the shots is in equal parts reassuring and frustrating. I decide to keep my mouth shut about it.

Grace thinks about it for a moment, before stepping aside and pulling me out of the doorway as well. "Okay, but you can't make Mom cry again."

Great. She's running my love life now. Well, I suppose she runs the rest of my life too, so it's only fitting.

"I won't." Daniel looks up at me now and mouths an apology. I'm unprepared for what I see in his eyes. That old photograph he shared last Saturday—his current state isn't far off.

The dark circles under his eyes, the puffiness. It's obvious that he's been suffering. Still is, maybe. I probably look very similar, which Grace noticed, evidently. She's so observant for a six-year-old.

"Why?" Grace asks.

Her question is met with silence, which grows heavier by the second until he closes the door behind himself. I want to invite him into the living room, but Grace isn't budging. She wants an answer, right now, in this cramped hallway.

"Grace, sweetheart, sometimes grownups make mistakes. Really big mistakes, much bigger than what kids make. Sometimes we say stuff we don't really mean, or we don't say stuff we should have said…" Daniel looks up at me. "All because we get scared and don't know how to handle it or talk about it."

"You get scared too?" Grace asks.

"Yep. I got scared, and I didn't know how to tell your mom about it, so instead I avoided her."

"But you're so… *old!* Like Mom."

That's too much even for me, and I can't suppress a little chuckle. Daniel kneels down next to her and rubs her shoulder. "I'm really sorry, Grace. Part of growing up is to own up to your mistakes and try to do better."

"I don't get so scared if I have Ed with me. And now, Max as well. 'Cos then nothing can hurt me."

"Max?" Daniel asks, looking up at me.

"The crocodile," I whisper.

"Right. That's a good name for him, well done!"

SEALED WITH A KISS

Grace wraps her arms around Daniel and hugs him against her. It would have been a heartwarming sight, if not for the circumstances that led up to this moment.

"Is it okay if I talk to your mom alone now, sweetheart? I have a lot to apologize to her for."

"Ummm… okay!" Grace lets him go and leaves us to it without further argument. I'm a little jealous he got her to give in so easily.

I don't know how to act around him now that we're alone, how to be. So I just stand there, with my arms hanging limp and my shoulders drooping. I'm so shattered. So wrung out. Do I have it in me to make it through the conversation we so desperately need?

I don't even ask him inside anymore. We stay in that little hallway, surrounded by coats and shoes and the colorful little backpack Grace carries to school with her.

"We can't be long. It's a weekday and I have to get Grace into bed soon," I mumble.

He doesn't speak, not right away. It makes me doubt if I ever said that out loud, and so I just end up staring at him blankly.

"I promised I'd never hurt Grace or you. I also promised you honesty, and I broke both those promises by pulling away," Daniel says, filling the silence. "I don't know how to appropriately apologize for that, but believe me. I am so, so sorry. It's all my fault."

I can see that he's upset. The way his mouth trembles when he speaks. But I don't have the energy to react appropriately. It's like I'm not really here.

"Things moved too quickly. We weren't ready for it. Shit happens." I feel numb. I'm still not sure I even want to have this conversation. It's too raw. Too difficult. Stirs up too many things I don't want to feel.

He shakes his head. "It's not that. Everything that happened leading up to Sunday evening was exactly how it should have been. All of it felt right. Natural."

I stare up at him, waiting for the hammer to fall. Yes, it was great one minute. And then it wasn't. And I'm not entirely sure I buy the 'I was scared' reasoning he gave to Grace. He was just trying to pacify her so we could get a moment alone. I don't know what he's planning to say that would make anything okay again. Because right now, nothing is. Least of all, me.

"What happened had nothing at all to do with you, and everything to do with me," Daniel says, averting his gaze. "I fucked up, excuse my language."

Ah, the old 'it's not you, it's me' excuse. That's enough to trigger me out of my earlier apathy.

"From one day to the next, you blew me off and then disappeared! You wouldn't even answer the phone!" I say.

A lump develops in my throat, which makes my voice heavier. As hard as I tried not to let him get to me, here we are. "One slightly awkward conversation, and that was it for you. And now you're back and I'm supposed to overlook what happened?"

He glances at me and I can see that his eyes are moist. Oh well, so are mine. Because what I really want to do is scream. I want to grab him, shake him up, and scream in his face.

You left me!

You abandoned me!

After telling me that you loved me and wouldn't hurt me, you did it anyway! And you can't tell me that it's on you and not on me, because this isn't the first time this has happened. This keeps happening. This is my own personal hell. Men keep leaving when I open up to them!

In the end, all I am is alone.

"No, you can't overlook that. I have no excuse. I have reasons, of course. But they don't excuse what I—" Daniel runs his hand through his messier-than-normal beard while continuing to stare at the empty space between us.

"I opened my life—my heart—to you and you left," I whisper, almost inaudibly.

He heard it, though, because I can see him shrink away. "Words can't express how sorry I am."

I don't respond. I don't know how to. All I want to do is cry, but I've done that already in the car, before picking Grace up from daycare, so I'm feeling wrung out and empty as a result.

"When Grace showed me her room, after making me promise not to tell you, she showed me a photograph—" Daniel says.

I frown and shake my head. What's that got to do with anything?

"—of her dad."

Of course. And that sparked his jealousy. That's why he started asking about Blake immediately after I put her to bed! But I'm not about that. I'm unwilling to talk about my ex to a new guy, only to be told I have too much baggage when he leaves. Except, he bolted anyway!

"That's no secret. When there's a child, there's bound to have been someone who fathered that child," I say, going from hurt to irritated again in a split second.

"Obviously. But I didn't expect to recognize—"

I look up at him, frowning. "You, *what?*"

"Look. I'm sorry, I've come to realize that I should have been upfront about this, but I didn't know how to broach the subject. I *know* him. From my past."

"How the hell do you know Blake? We were together for four whole years. I knew *all* of his friends and yet I'd never seen you before."

"We weren't friends. And it's a long time ago; twenty-two years in all. Long before you and him— But in a way, when I saw his picture, it hit me like it was only yesterday." Daniel's demeanor changes again. And when he glances up at me now, I recognize the look in his eyes all too well. This wasn't jealousy. Whatever it is, it runs so much deeper. There's the old him from the photo I couldn't stand to look at. There's the despair I recognized from my own past.

It frightens me and makes me take a step back, with my heart suddenly hammering in my throat again. It takes me a couple of minutes, just to formulate a sentence. A whole two minutes, which we spend staring at each other, stunned.

"What did Blake do to you?" My question seems to echo in the silence that remains when I complete it. All I can hear is the blood rushing in my ears.

Then he inhales deeply, pauses, and exhales. And the whole atmosphere in the room seems to shift. There's a tickle in the pit of my throat. Just for a second; just before he replies.

"What *didn't* he do?" Daniel says.

Now I can breathe again. Yeah. Same.

"So when I asked you about him, and you wouldn't tell me anything, I wondered if maybe..." his voice trails off.

I shake my head. *What?*

"I wondered if you still had feelings..."

Fury rushes through me like a flash flood. "Feelings? For *that* asshole?"

"Well…" Daniel deflates further, which is hard to do for a man of his stature. "That answers that. And I broke my promises and ruined everything we had for absolutely no reason."

Exasperated, I throw my hands up in the air. "I was trying to be civil! I was trying not to badmouth my ex, who also happens to be my little girl's father. So that I wouldn't put you off with all the bullshit from my past. I was trying—"

"I'm so sorry. I let my own history catch up with me. I honestly thought I was over it."

I'm trembling now. Completely overcome. My knees shake, as do my shoulders. I can hardly stand to look at him anymore.

"Yeah, so did I, but then another man leaves me and I'm right back there!" I cry out. "No matter what I do, I'm always back in the same place! Alone!"

Tears are streaming down my face. I don't have the energy to hold them back anymore. What's the use, anyway? All week I've fought so hard not to cry at home, and Gracie still noticed something was up. She still felt she had to take care of me. Protect me. I'm such a failure.

"I'm *so* sorry," he says. "So, very sorry."

You said that already.

"Every time I think it's going to be different! How many times can a person keep on hoping?" I sob. Ugh, this is so uncalled for. I'm a fucking mess. No wonder nobody stuck around so far. I'd run away from me too if I could.

I hide my face in my hands, but it's just no use trying to stop the flood anymore. It's rushing through me, shaking my whole body right to its core.

"You kept trying to tell me. And I didn't hear you," Daniel says.

One of his hands gently rests on my shoulder. The sensation in my skin is so intense, it almost hurts. Actually, it's my heart that's hurting. I don't have the will to shake him off.

"All the times she asked where her dad was… And if she did something wrong to make him leave…" A deep shudder passes through my back. Never before have I told anyone about this. *Never.* Because I was too afraid of letting all this ugliness out. Because I *know* how that feels. I've spent half of my life asking myself these same questions ever since *my* dad—

"Oh I still have feelings alright! I hate his guts for what he did to us. To *her!*" I say. "We never would have worked out as a couple, but he's still her dad… He still should've—" I can't finish the sentence, I can only sob.

Daniel's hand tugs at me, nudging me forward, until his other arm surrounds me too. I cling to him. Not sure why, but it feels right. I wrap my arms around him and hide my face in his chest to muffle my cries. Though Gracie has probably heard me already. I've done a shit job of protecting her from this mess so far. God. I'm a terrible mother.

"I didn't mean to repeat his mistakes! I didn't mean to—" He caresses my back, trying to soothe me, but it's wooden and awkward. Oh God. I'm really freaking him out now. I've lost all self respect.

"I'm so sorry. This is inappropriate. I'm being dramatic," I sniffle and try to retreat, but he doesn't let me go. He keeps holding onto me, giving me no choice but to stay put.

"Fuck, that's why everyone keeps saying to communicate, to listen! I jumped to conclusions and it sent me into a pit of despair. I couldn't function. I didn't know what to say to you to explain it," he stammers.

I realize that *he's* the one who is shivering and trembling now. He's a mess too. And that kills me all over again, and makes me switch roles. I wiggle free of his embrace, just enough to be able to bring my face up closer to his and wrap one of my arms around his neck and shoulders.

"Tell me," I say.

This is the hardest conversation I've ever had to have. The most painful. Perhaps this is where we needed to go together. This is the depth we needed to explore, so that maybe, we'll emerge on the other side better and stronger than before. *Maybe*—

"I thought…" he starts, then pauses to take a deep

breath. I close my eyes and wait. And while I do so, I try to make sense of all these confusing emotions coursing through me. Can he feel them too? Probably, that's why he's so broken up as well. What a couple of sad sacks we are.

"All I've wanted all along was to be—"

"Enough," I complete his sentence, opening my eyes again. He wanted to be enough. I know, because it's what I've always wanted too.

He squeezes his arm around me. "Yeah. And after spending almost the whole weekend together. I thought I had found everything I could ever want. The two of you are a dream come true. The family I've always yearned for. And you've been so welcoming, so—"

"Then Gracie showed you that picture," I mumble.

"I convinced myself that *he* was the one you really wanted. That he'd taken this dream away from me too."

That sounds so ludicrous, it's almost funny. Only, it's not. Rather than follow my initial impulse and swallow my true feelings, I fight like hell to express them. I fight like hell, for the honesty I've been craving from him, which I've failed to give him so far.

"If I never have to see his face again, I'll die a happy woman," I confess. This one hurts too. Right there in my heart. Because it feels wrong to wish that, for Gracie's sake.

"He hurt you way worse than he ever hurt me," Daniel concludes. "And he almost destroyed me back in the day. Then he almost did it again this week."

Taking a moment to let his words sink in, I realize I'm not angry anymore. I'm not so afraid anymore either, even if my heart is still racing. Because if Daniel found the courage to come halfway across town to my door to clear the air with me in his current state. And if after I exposed all the mess I feel inside to him, his first reaction was to hold me... To give me space to fall apart and try to catch me... Then, maybe...

Maybe I wasn't wrong to love him.

He has issues, and they're not all in the past as he himself had wanted to believe. Hell, I have some pretty major issues too, which came bubbling to the surface just now. And we spoke up. We confessed. That's huge, and we just did it *together*.

We admitted our biggest fears to each other. Laid ourselves bare. I could have never done that with any other man; certainly not fucking Blake, who never seemed to give a shit about how I felt even when we were together. I tried with one or two others, but they bolted at the first opportunity.

But I just did it with Daniel, and he accepted me. Just as I accepted him. That realization fills me with a kind of bravery I've never felt before. This isn't a warm and fuzzy hug to mark the end of a romantic date. This isn't the crowning glory on some happy-go-lucky walk at the botanical gardens. This is reality. This is truth. This is honesty. And all the ugliness that goes along with it.

I lean back, cup his face, and press my lips against his. Both our faces, still stained with tears, merge. And we kiss. We kiss like our lives depend on it.

They probably do. What are the chances of us getting together like this? Two people, with a common thread in our past, which affected us so deeply, no one else could ever hope to understand.

His kisses are hungry, desperate. I notice that mine are too. I couldn't stop if I wanted to.

This is right. This is what we are meant to do.

"I don't expect—" Our lips continue to seek each other out after every breathless word. "—you to forgive me."

I don't know what to say to that. So I just kiss him deeper. Because forgiveness isn't a thing anymore. Not now, when the pieces have fallen into place to reveal the whole picture.

I understand now. What he did wasn't malicious. Radio silence for a few days while he figures things out is hardly something to have to beg for forgiveness for.

But it wasn't my fault that I overreacted the way I did either. He triggered something in me I couldn't yet understand or control. That's life for you. Nobody gets through it unscathed or unchanged. You just have to try to make sense of your stupid impulses when they happen.

If only we can keep this going, and we can stay honest and open with each other, we'll make it. Together: it's him and me against the world. Or at least against the Blakes of the world. Because, seriously, and I don't care anymore that he's Gracie's dad: fuck that guy. In hindsight, it doesn't surprise me that he was a terror in his younger days too and hurt a gentle soul like Daniel. That's completely on brand for Blake.

I was young and stupid when we got together. Didn't think I deserved better than him, even when he let me and later Grace down repeatedly. Even when he hurt me.

But I *do* deserve better. And so does Daniel. Maybe we can be better together?

In between our feverish affections, I pull away just for a second to look into his eyes. His beautifully deep, once again unguarded eyes. Together, we can learn to be better to each other as well as ourselves.

I should have just talked to him on Sunday.

"I don't need apologies. I need to know you're with me," I say.

He visibly tenses up, but he doesn't evade my gaze. *It was all my fault.*

"With me and Grace," I correct myself.

"I'm with you. Forever. No matter what."

I smile briefly, and yet another tear rolls down my cheek. Because looking at him now, I believe him. It took guts to come here and face us. To admit to everything that's been going through his mind. He couldn't know how him distancing himself would affect me, because I never said anything. I never explained that my dad left my mom and me years before I gave Blake the chance to repeat the cycle. And every other man since.

I didn't tell him, so he couldn't know. That's on me, not him. I was just too afraid that he'd see what they saw and do the same. Too afraid of not being enough myself. If only I'd been honest like I wanted to be! I could have saved both of us so much heartache.

"Please don't disappear on us again," I say instead.

"Never again," he confirms. There's honesty in his eyes. And that's all that matters.

"If you ever need space again, just say so. I'll wait for you," I add.

He shakes his head. "You won't have to wait. Because I'm not going anywhere."

Those words bring tears to my eyes all over again. Because I can see he means it. I can see the love in his eyes. He's really trying. So I'll really try too. I owe it to the both of us.

"I missed you so much," Daniel whispers, while wrapping his arms around me again.

Oh hell, me too. So very much.

CHAPTER SIXTEEN

* Daniel *

When I arrived here I knew it was my last stand. I had nothing left to lose. But now, I might have gained even more than I could ever predict. After she invites me in and we both settle down on the couch, for much of the time, we don't even talk anymore. There's nothing much to say, at least in words.

I confessed my fears about Kate's past with Blake earlier, and she really listened. Through her tears and her own pain and fear, she actually stopped and tried to understand my perspective.

Nobody has ever done that for me willingly. *No one.*

And then she reached out and kissed me, and I fell even harder than before. And although my thoughts still were racing, and I was on the verge of losing my nerve all over again, I tried to focus on her. How she looked. How she smelled. How she felt.

It helped me ignore my inner voice, telling me what a failure I am. How badly I fucked up. How I don't deserve her forgiveness, and I should die alone in a hole somewhere.

Negative self-talk, Owen had called it. That sounds

a lot tamer than it actually is.

And it's not like Owen told me anything new. The all-or-nothing thinking; the catastrophizing; those things I know about already. Because I've tried so many times to rationalize myself out of these cycles. And sometimes it even worked.

But this week, I got blindsided. And it was entirely unnecessary.

All those stories I told myself about Kate and Blake; all those nightmare scenarios were just that. They weren't real. I see it in her eyes when she talks about him now. The scars he left in her run deep. That's why she wouldn't answer my questions about him on Sunday.

Owen was right. She hadn't dealt with her past with him either.

If I've learned anything, it's that I won't pry again. I won't force those memories open for her, and I won't jump to conclusions either. How can I? Throughout our entire conversation I couldn't bring myself to tell her the details of everything I've been reliving either. I've hinted at some things. Even that was almost too much.

Even now, it's still so raw and painful. Even as every caress and kiss and embrace from her tries to soothe it, it's still bleeding. Because you can't fix a depressive episode with a single conversation, no matter how meaningful or deep. I know now that's what this is. My mind has been playing tricks on me so convincingly that I let it happen again. There's no switch to be flipped. No secret code to be input to defuse it again…

But she's here, in my arms. I can feel her. The warmth of her body against mine. The silkiness of her hair pressed up against the side of my face. Most of all, I feel the firmness of her hands on me. Telling me that she's serious. She wants me here. She doesn't want to let go, and neither do I.

I could cry some more. Like an absolute loser. But I don't.

Because she's with me. And I'm with her. That's what I keep telling myself to drown out what remains of the darkness in my mind.

She missed me. She wants me here. She—

"I love you," she tells me every so often. I make sure to tell her the same. Again and again. Maybe that way we'll both end up believing it.

I don't know how much time has passed. Minutes? Hours? While we remain entwined in each other's arms on the sofa, just*existing*. What I do know is that with every passing moment my inner critic gets a little quieter. A little less convincing. Every time she tells me she loves me, that negative voice in my mind talks back a little less.

"Mom?"

Kate tenses up in my arms and I freeze.

"Mom, are you okay?" Grace asks.

Kate sighs and leans back a little, but she doesn't fully retreat. She doesn't release me. Just as well, because I would have lost my shit all over again. I look up, tentatively, and see her smile at her little girl, who is standing only a couple of feet away from us, clutching the comically large stuffed crocodile to her chest.

"Come here, sweet pea." Kate waves her over.

"It's my bedtime, remember?" Grace asks.

My heart sinks. I made Kate miss tucking in her little girl. That's despicable.

"Right you are. And you're already wearing your jammies too! I'm so very proud of you."

"Well, I've got school in the morning, so I can't be up too late…" Grace explains while wrapping her arms around Kate's neck and crawling up onto her thigh.

They both look up at me and I'm still frozen.

"Are you okay?" Grace asks me. "If you're still scared, you can borrow Max for a while."

I glance down at the toy she's presenting to me, and back at her face, then at Kate, who's biting her bottom lip and trying really hard to keep it together.

"Sweetheart, I'm fine," I tell her. "I was just—"

She reaches for me with one arm, and Kate with the other. I hug both of them and the toy, sandwiched in between us. My eyes shut naturally as

I'm overwhelmed with a comforting warmth. I could stay like this forever. Kate sighs deeply, as does Grace, barely a second later.

We remain as we are for a few more seconds, when I realize that all is quiet now. Gone is the constant chattering in my mind. All that remains is calm.

"I love both of you," I say. More than life itself.

Kate's hand on my back twitches briefly, then tightens around me. I find myself smiling. I almost forgot what that felt like. This past week, I very nearly forgot what it was like to *feel*.

"Mom," Grace chirps up.

"Yes, sweet pea?"

"He said he's sorry, so it's okay now, right?" she asks.

I chuckle softly and caress her hair.

"That's right. Things are okay now."

Grace looks up at Kate, then back at me again, when her expression goes solemn and thoughtful all of a sudden.

"In that case, I think it would be okay if you get married, like Ms. Lawson and her boyfriend. Just as long as you promise to be nice to each other from now on."

I nearly choke on my own breath. When my eyes meet Kate's, I see she's equally shocked at Grace's statement.

"I'm sorry, I think it's a bit early—" Kate stammers, then mouths a 'sorry' at me.

It is too early. And unexpected. And… And it also feels absolutely right. Though I would have liked to bring up this topic under entirely different circumstances. *From the mouths of babes,* as they say. I find myself grinning from ear to ear after her comment, even if I can't quite get a word out.

"I think it's time we get you tucked in now, young lady!" Kate firmly tells Grace.

Moments earlier, the prospect of letting either of them go would have been too painful to contemplate. But now… I watch as Kate gets Grace up and ushers her across the living room, towards the hallway. And I can't help but smile some more. She is quite something. Both of them are, quite possibly, *everything.*

"Goodnight, Gracie. Sweet dreams!" I call after her.

"Goodnight, Daniel!" She gives me a little wave, then turns around and takes Kate's hand while walking out of the room.

"I think he's nice, Mom. I don't think he'll do it again," I overhear her telling Kate. Well, if that isn't the best seal of approval I could ever hope for…

She may not be my daughter, and I've only met her briefly so far, but I already know I'd do anything for her. For both of them, actually. I can't imagine anything less. Just how Blake-fucking-Callahan made the decision to walk out on them, I'll never understand.

His loss is my luck. If he hadn't, I would have never known this feeling I feel right now. The deep, fundamental sense of belonging and pride I felt while I had them both in my arms together. The feeling of contentment still lingers even after I'm left in the living room by myself.

*** Kate ***

I try not to rush it. Try not to just dump Grace in her room so that I can rush back to Daniel. It's hard, though. It's impossible to know where his mind is after Grace brought up marriage, of all things.

Jesus. This child has no filter! No understanding of the thought and care adult relationships demand. It's not just as simple as: he's nice, let's get married! I'm going to have to clear up this insanity as soon as I get her to finish brushing her teeth and settle down in bed. I wouldn't want him to get cold feet over something that wasn't even on my mind yet at all!

We only just started dating! We've literally just had our first big conflict, and hopefully resolved it. And now…

I watch as Gracie rinses and puts her toothbrush away, all without prompting or reminders. Afterwards, I let her lead me into her bedroom, and try to stay as patient and calm as I can while I help her climb into bed.

Though, Daniel did tell me earlier that he would be there for us. Forever. That's as much of a commitment as anyone could ask for. But surely that doesn't mean—

"You be a good girl now and sleep, okay?" I tell Grace, while pulling the covers up over her and Ed, the octopus, to her left, and Max, the crocodile, to her right. She has her eyes tightly shut and pretends not to hear me anymore.

"Goodnight, sweet pea." I lean down and brush a few errant locks of hair aside before kissing her on her forehead.

She is the best kid anyone could ever hope for. Despite her big mouth. She doesn't know any better… And I hope she never loses that innocence either. The longer she carries on believing in happily-ever-afters, the better.

"Nighty night!" I tell her, while switching off the light and lingering in her room for another couple of seconds just to admire her.

Daniel said he loved both of us. I know that he meant it. In her case, how could he not? She's the literal best.

I tiptoe out of the room and carefully close the door behind me. Even though I know there's no chance she could have fallen asleep the very moment her head hit the pillow. Still. This is the game we play every day. No reason to change that now.

What *has* changed tonight is that I'm not heading back to an otherwise empty living room after tucking her in. There's Daniel, and all the relationship talk we still have to clear up after Grace's wildly inappropriate remarks.

My heart is racing again when I open the door and find him already looking at me.

"She's asleep?"

"Pretending to be, anyway," I tell him, with an apologetic smile.

I pause in the doorway for a moment, prompting him to get up and walk a couple of steps towards me.

"Should I head home? It is a school night, after all," he asks.

I quickly shake my head. Sending him home is the last thing on my mind. Not now, when I just got him back.

A part of me, the irrational part that believes in fairytales still, doesn't want him to ever leave. That part just wants to curl up in his arms again and stay there forever. 'Til death do us part.

Ugh. Here I go again. So suggestible. Am I really going to let Grace's remarks steer my love life for me?

I rest my hand on the side of his face and really study him. At the dark circles under his eyes which I'd spotted earlier. And the stubble that's grown outside of his normally very well kept and trimmed beard. And the glimmer of insecurity I see in him, which reminds me of how terrified he looked when I opened the door on him. It's that last observation which finally makes me open my mouth again and tell the truth like I always should have done in the first place. How much pain could have been avoided if I'd just—

"I know that it's way too early for any of this, but… I don't want you to go. I *never* want you to go," I say.

There's a tremble in his bottom lip, just for a second, before he wraps his arms around me again. It reminds me of the observation I made during our third date at the coffee shop. About how terrible he is at hearing anything nice being said to him. About how I vowed to myself to keep on doing exactly that until he's able to hear a compliment without flinching.

"And I'm so sorry I wouldn't answer your questions about Blake on Sunday," I say.

He sighs. "I should have respected your wishes and backed off."

"Perhaps. But I shouldn't have kept his secrets for him either."

"Tell me whenever you're ready. Or don't tell me. It doesn't matter anymore, as long as we continue to be there for each other," Daniel says.

That sounds like a trick. I lean back to look him in

the eye again. His expression looks completely genuine. Can we truly resolve everything with just one conversation about it, and brush the rest of the truth aside?

What if it turns out *he* doesn't have time for my bullshit either, if I open up the rest of the way? Like the other men in my life before? What if the real me isn't in fact enough for him?

Then again, what if the tables were turned? If he chooses to share all the ugliness of his past with me, would I run? I'm certain that I would never, no matter what he'd say. I would be honored to hear every detail.

"I *want* to tell you everything about me," I conclude. *Maybe one day, you'll tell me everything too.*

He tightens his embrace on me and nuzzles my hair. When I close my eyes, and let his scent fill my lungs all the way, it makes me smile again. Because here, I'm at home. Here, I am safe.

Now that we've found our way back to each other, I realize that I do trust him. I was already more attracted to him than anyone who's ever come before. And we haven't even slept together yet. Is that weird?

There's a stupid dating rule I remember, which says you're supposed to have sex after the third date. I'm not sure if tonight counts as our fifth, which makes us well overdue. Then again, we don't do stupid dating rules. We forge our own path.

I totally *would*, though. I've been wanting to since Saturday.

"Do you want to stay the night?" I ask, while leaning back a little to make eye contact with him again. *Please say yes.*

He hesitates for a second. "I would literally follow you to the end of the world. That said, I do have to let Jack out at some point tonight, or he may end up destroying my carpet."

I chuckle awkwardly. Of course; the dog. How silly of me.

"For a while, then?" I ask.

"Wish I could, though. Stay the whole night." He glances down at my lips, letting his gaze linger there. The resulting tension I feel is making me forget myself.

This time I don't make a move. I stay exactly where I am, feeling the buzz of electricity that fills the air.

There are but inches between us. I can feel him; his presence; his heat.

My body is reacting with a mind of its own.

But I won't go first. Not this time. The best things come to those who wait…

CHAPTER SEVENTEEN

* Daniel *

I can't stay the night, no matter how badly I want to. Those big pleading eyes could convince me of anything, just not animal cruelty. I can't leave Jack alone for that long. Kate looks hurt when I tell her so. Maybe even a little fearful.

"For a while, then?" she asks. She looks so small and vulnerable in my arms.

"Wish I could, though. Stay the whole night," I tell her. As well as every night going forward.

That seems to reassure her. And anyway, I can definitely stay for about half of it. I wouldn't cut it any shorter than it needs to be for Jack's sake.

For a while, I can't stop staring at her beautiful full lips. Rose pink, like some of the flowers in bloom at Kew Gardens, where we walked after our second date. The longer I look, the more I want to kiss them again. And again. And the rest of her too.

I let the excitement bubble up in me. To soothe all the anxiety and doom and gloom of the past few days. And for once I'm not thinking about whether I'm doing it right. Or where to put my hands, or how our size difference might make things awkward. Or if I'm even supposed to touch her at all.

She asked for me to stay. In her home. All night.

I'm invited. I'm wanted.

Despite everything that happened this week. Everything I did wrong and all the ways I inadvertently hurt her.

I'm still wanted. What a feeling; to not be punished for your mistakes but to be forgiven instead. She's shown me something new yet again.

I cup her beautiful face with both hands. More gently and carefully than the last time I stole a kiss like this at the zoo. That was the *before* time. This is now, after we've come closer to each other than ever before. I want to cherish this.

I take my time, looking into her expressive eyes, inhaling her intoxicating scent and finally leaning down and letting our lips touch.

The electricity that sparks between us takes my breath away. Just like that, she seems to give me life.

All my predictions for this moment turned out to be wrong.

I thought that if I apologized for my behavior and explained myself, even if she accepted it, I'd feel differently about us. That I would no longer melt a little every time she tells me she loves me. That I'd unmask those words as lies and wishful thinking and fantasy. That this honeymoon feeling would be gone forever, because she could never mean it.

Because I couldn't possibly be worthy.

But those were just idle fears; more of my own mind, playing tricks on me. And my heart was never on the same page about any of it. My heart still wanted to believe. That's why it hurt so much. I was torn in opposing directions.

I still love her all the same. Actually, I love her more now. Because now, she's seen me nearly at my worst. And she didn't tell me to suck it up or snap out of it. She didn't ridicule me or tell me not to be such a baby. She didn't close the door on me and send me away, although she had every right and opportunity to.

Instead, she pulled back the curtain on herself and expressed her own biggest fear. The one I accidentally triggered when I sent her that stupid lie of a message on Monday.

And it's actually the same as mine. She's just as afraid of rejection and abandonment as I am.

My mind is blown. So is my heart. Because I know what to do now. I just don't leave her. I don't give up, so that she doesn't have to either. She's been hurt deeply in the past. By Blake, for sure. And from the sounds of it, others too. I can't imagine why, because to me, she's perfect. Any man would be lucky to stand by her side.

All I have to do to make this right is not to repeat their mistakes. I just have to be there for her. I just have to stay.

And I have to show her I mean it. With my words, with my mouth, and my hands… I just have to follow my instincts and hold her, just like I did when she broke down in front of me. I just have to *love* her.

That, I can do. Gladly. For the rest of my life.

And so I carry on loving her right now. With my arms wrapped around her, I enjoy every second of our reunion. Her body pressed up against me, making me feel yet more things I've never experienced before.

Her hands on me, keeping me close, making my heart race out of control.

Her tongue, dancing around mine, teasing me as well as tasting me. And letting me taste her.

I've never been so turned on in my life. My head is spinning and the blood is rushing in my ears, drowning out any other sound in the room. Yet it still feels so natural. So right.

I stumble backwards towards the sofa. Or does she direct me there? I don't know.

Even while settling down, I can't bring myself to stop touching her. Her hands are on me too. My shoulders. My chest. My hair.

She straddles me, and I forget to breathe.

My right hand ends up on her hip, then wraps around her lower back, pressing her up into me, unwilling to ever let go.

She moans into my lips, and I'm about ready to explode right then and there. Jesus. How do I stop this train after it's already been set in motion?

"I love you," I whisper. "God, I love you."

And she whispers the same magic words back at me, into my parted lips.

It's amazingly, mind-blowingly intense.

"You're so perfect," I tell her. "So beautiful. Stunning…"

"You too."

No. No, I'm not. But she doesn't allow me the time to protest, because her lips are on mine again.

"I'm ready for the next step," she whispers, the next time she comes up for air. Her fingers hook teasingly into the collar of my t-shirt, tugging at it just enough to make her point.

Holy shit, what do I do now? How does this magical dream end? I mean… I've thought about it. Fantasized about it pretty obsessively these last couple of weeks. But that was just that, a dream. Whereas *this*…

"Whenever you want," she adds, biting her bottom lip for a second. "No pressure."

They were pink earlier. They're red now, after all our kisses. And her eyes… I've never seen her look at me like this. Hungry, like I'm everything she desires.

This, I never dared to dream of. It seemed too far-fetched. Too out of this world. And also too confronting. Because the possibilities for how this situation could progress… they stir something else up in me.

The same ugly fear that reared its head on Saturday.

What if…

What if she doesn't look at me like this anymore once our clothes come off, but instead… What if I recognize the disappointment on her face?

No, I'm being negative again… Owen would have a field day with me if he knew what I was thinking now.

"What's wrong?" Kate leans back, looking down at me with her hands on either side of my face.

"Nothing. Everything is exactly how—"

She shakes her head. "I can feel it. Something's off."

I tighten my arms around her waist and focus on how that feels. God, she's amazing. This whole situation is surreal.

"What if Grace wakes up?" I ask her.

She pauses for a moment. "There's a lock on the bedroom door."

We stare at each other for a moment. My heart continues to race, and I'm starting to sweat a little now. But the longer I carry on looking into her eyes, the braver I feel. I'm wanted. For whatever reason, she wants this as much as I do.

SEALED WITH A KISS

"Let's go," I whisper.

The corner of her mouth twitches into a quick smile as she gets off me. I reluctantly let her go, but then she grabs my hand, prompting me into action as well. We tiptoe through the hall past Gracie's room and into the master bedroom like naughty teenagers. She makes a beeline for the bed, while I take a moment, catching my breath, and turn the key on the door lock as silently as I can.

That was dishonest of me. A valid concern, but still not what was holding me back.

I turn to look at her, reclining against the pillows, observing me.

"You're beautiful," I tell her.

She smiles and gestures at me to join her. I want to. I want nothing more.

But what I really meant to say was 'you're too beautiful for me'.

"You're perfection, and I'm—" *A work in progress that will never be finished,* I try to say, but I don't complete that thought. This is pathetic. She doesn't want to hear any of this. I'm killing the mood.

She briefly shakes her head, still looking up at me, expectantly. "We can just kiss. And cuddle."

I don't want to *cuddle.* I mean, yeah I do. But I want so much more! Then why is this so damn hard?

Finally, I force myself to approach the bed and join her. When she reaches for me, wrapping her arms around my neck, I can breathe freely again. With my forehead pressed up against hers, I find my balance.

"These last few days without you have been hell," I confess.

"For me too."

"I'm so sorry," I say.

"So am I."

She kisses me, and I kiss her, and somehow, I end up on my back, with her draped on top of me. And it's the best feeling in the world. And then she grabs me, tugging at me to turn, and we switch roles, with me on top of her. And that's even better.

And then, in between more breathless affections, she slips her hand into the back of my t-shirt, caressing the bare skin underneath, and I could die a little. I open my eyes to look at her, and I'm simply in awe of what I see.

Because she can feel everything I've been worried about. There's no hiding it. I'm not as in shape as I would have wanted to be. Far from it. And she doesn't hesitate.

When she opens her eyes, she doesn't look any less turned on than she did earlier.

"You feel so good!" she whispers against my lips.

Do I? She surely does, though. Everything about her is perfection.

I lean up on one elbow, and peel her top off her

side just enough for me to get my hand in. She arches her back, allowing me access underneath. I was entirely unprepared for the softness of her skin. And so I kiss her again. Not her lips this time, but the side of her neck, as well as every bit of flesh the neckline of her top exposes, down to her clavicle. I did this once before and she seemed to like it then…

She whimpers my name and digs her fingernails into my shoulder blade. It's too much. Too fast. I can't stop.

The sound of fabric, tearing, fills the room. I'm not sure where it came from or what it was, until I feel a tickle of air against my back.

I lean up on both elbows, looking down at her.

"You tore my shirt," I tell her.

She doesn't say a word, doesn't move a muscle, just stares at me.

"You tore it!" I repeat, chuckling awkwardly.

She purses her lips. "Well… I guess it's too late now."

"What?"

Her eyes narrow defiantly, and her body tenses, and the sound repeats, much louder than before. And there is yet more air touching me from somewhere at the back.

"Oh hell no!" I say, while somehow balancing on my elbows just right to hook my fingers into the neckline of her top and tugging at it until it gives way too.

She lets out a little giggle. It's infectious, because it makes me chuckle too. And then she laughs, before covering her mouth to muffle it. Even so, it's the most beautiful sound I've ever heard.

* Kate *

"You tore it!"

For a second, I nearly lose it. It was an accident; I got carried away, desperate to get closer to him physically. Although he sounds shocked, the heat in his eyes still remains. And I don't know what comes over me, but I don't backtrack. I double down. I put all my strength into it, and tear his t-shirt all the way in half.

It's an act of rebellion. An act of protest. Maybe it's revenge for all the hurt I've felt over the past few days.

Whatever it is, it's just what he needed to get over himself already before retaliating.

He rips my top from the neckline down, and the expectant look in his eyes makes me laugh. Because this moment is too bizarre. It's weird and childish and totally unlike me. And it's so much fun. Like the two of us taking our shoes off and walking barefoot through Kew Gardens after our second date.

"Now we're even," I tell him, my eyes moist with tears of laughter.

He shakes his head, grinning widely at me. "What the hell am I supposed to wear when I head home later?"

"You're a guy. You can go topless. It's still warm out!" I tell him.

He laughs, which makes me laugh again, until he steals a glance downward, and pauses.

"God, you really are incredibly beautiful," he says.

Before he realizes what's going on, I pull the remnants of his t-shirt off, until they're just hanging there around his arms. And the view that awaits me doesn't disappoint either.

I'm such a sucker for broad, hairy chests and thick, strong arms, and Daniel delivers on all fronts. I love everything I see and feel and can't stop treating myself to the view.

He catches me and freezes.

I tentatively place my hand on the center of his chest, where the hair is densest.

"You're gorgeous," I say. "Like a great big sexy teddy bear!"

Or a hot lumberjack. A protector. A provider. Everything that I remember thinking about when I first saw him in the video Claire sent. He keeps telling me I'm perfect, but I'm not. *He* is. I never even told anyone about my preferences. Not even Claire. But she knew my type even better than I did myself. How right she was to set us up together. Not just the physical, but all the other stuff is perfect too. The weird overlap in our past. The similar struggles we had to go through to get to where we are now. All of it.

How could she know?

I'm in dad bod heaven.

"You don't mind?" he asks.

Claire knew, but Daniel still has no clue.

I smile up at him. "Mind? You're so exactly my type, it's almost unnerving!"

He exhales sharply. "I just thought, because Blake—"

I shake my head. "He was never right for me. We had no chemistry. He was just the sort of guy I *thought* I was supposed to date. Biggest regret of my life, if not for Gracie."

He doesn't argue, but I can tell he's still unconvinced. And so I take a deep breath and try to hype myself up to be open. Just be honest.

"Remember when I told you about Claire sending me your video before all this?"

He nods.

"It wasn't random. She reached out to me for a reason. She already knew I'd like you. That we'd be a match, in every possible way. And she didn't need questionnaires and surveys and whatever-that-guy's-name-is—"

"Owen."

"Yeah, him. She didn't need anything else to know that. Because she knows *me*. Better than I know myself sometimes. And she was spot on! I didn't do her a favor, she did me one!"

"Okay, but…" He glances down at himself. "You obviously take care of your appearance. And I—"

"Are you kidding me? And you don't? You didn't make sure to style your hair and trim your beard just right for every date we've been on, and wear just the right amount of cologne to smell nice without overdoing it… And are you about to tell me you don't go to the gym at least once a week? Because I can tell that you do!" I say, squeezing his arm to make my point. "And you clearly make sure to eat healthy, or else you wouldn't have lost a whole lot of weight these last few years. It would have been impossible otherwise."

He presses his lips together and takes a deep breath. I've hit a nerve.

"Right."

"I know you do all that, Daniel. I see you. You've worked damn hard on yourself to get to where you are," I say.

No fake smiles or waffling aimlessly or running away from the topic now. This is what I *should* have said when he showed me that picture on Saturday. This is my do-over.

"I love you. I love everything you are." I grab his

face and pull him into me for a kiss. "And what you are is fucking sexy. And I want you so bad I'm about to lose my mind."

"I want you too," he stammers. "I've been going crazy for you ever since…"

"Since that wild make-out session under the chestnut tree?"

He groans against my lips. "Before that too, but I've been dying for more ever since."

"I've dreamed about you, Daniel. Every single night."

His whole body seems to tense as he forces his hand underneath me, gathering me up into his arms and grinding his hips down into me simultaneously. It's the hottest thing ever. He's actually dying for what's next.

As am I.

CHAPTER EIGHTEEN

Here I am, in a situation which only a few years ago seemed impossibly out of reach. In bed, with the most beautiful woman I've ever laid eyes on. Her hands and lips all over me, trying to still the doubts I can't seem to shake.

I still am not sure I heard what she was trying to tell me just now. Or did I just imagine it?

Either way, what's happening between us right now doesn't require me to know for sure. Or to think. It's pure biology. Instinct.

I'm so fucking hard for her. Just her.

Never once have I felt this way before. Sure as hell not while watching porn. Not even in the filthiest possible dream.

I can't even stop myself from grinding into her. I'm completely out of control.

And she's right here with me. Her fingers dig into my bare shoulders, until one of her hands slides down, down, down and rests on the waistband of my jeans.

Before I know what's going on, she's in, grabbing my ass.

Lord have mercy. I can't. I just—

I freeze right there, panting for air as the inevitable is happening, without realizing exactly where my face has ended up. This can't be. I can't be done already!

She arches up into me, moaning softly. Searing heat comes off her cleavage, just below my mouth, getting me back on task.

I kiss her, lick her, nibble on her. Just because it feels right.

Goosebumps raise up against my lips. A similar shiver passes down my spine.

Or maybe that's because I'm still feeling exposed without my t-shirt on.

I haven't had my shirt off in front of someone in… The last time, in a school locker room didn't go so well.

But I'm not that kid anymore. Even if I just behaved like a bloody teenager and came way too early. I ought to be ashamed of myself. But… The calm that has washed over me is just too powerful for further doubts to break through.

I see you, she'd said, while listing all the ways in which I've tried to better myself. All the things I've tried which never seemed to be enough.

I want you.

Fuck. Those two things are almost better than all the times she told me she loves me. Almost, though not quite. They're better in conjunction with the knowledge that I have her love too.

It's a matter of trust. When I showed her that old photo of mine, she said she wouldn't judge me. I thought at the time that she did. That she looked disappointed. But maybe that was yet more evidence of my own doubts playing tricks on me.

I raise myself off her just enough to be able to see. She's already looking at me. Already waiting. What could I possibly do for her to make her feel as good as I feel right now? I swallow hard. I want to trust her. I do. She *won't* judge me.

"Teach me how to please you," I whisper.

Her eyes shut for a split second, as her breathing speeds up. So this is what female desire looks like. *Feels like*. I'll never tire of it.

"Start by loving me. The way you wish to be loved," she says.

A tough one. Because I don't know what I wish for. It was relief I craved earlier. And that's done now. I might be new at this, but I've read enough to know that there's more to it than that.

"I..." I want to—I need to—Words fail me, because I can't catch a deep breath.

"Caress me," she whispers. I can definitely do that.

Rolling onto my side next to her allows me to touch her better. She wriggles out of her torn top. It's hard to resist the urge to grab her breasts. Made impossible by the fact that she reaches behind herself and unclasps her bra, and…

Good lord, am I really allowed to be here and see her like this?

"Kiss me," she says, nodding downward.

Hell yes! Resting my hand on the dip of her waist, I lean into the same spot where I was resting my head earlier, and I inhale. I plant a thousand kisses on her chest. First in her cleavage, then across the swell of her breast, until my mouth reaches the reward in the center.

"Taste me," she breathes.

I don't need to be prompted again, because I just go for it. Closing my lips around her hard nipple, I lick her; tease her; tickle her. She reacts by grabbing my hair, keeping my lips exactly in place.

Her breaths have turned into low moans. And as I find my rhythm, she does too, grinding into me, her crotch against my thigh. She seems to enjoy that too. Enjoys it more when I let her hook her legs around mine, letting her apply more pressure.

She's the one rubbing against me now. Harder and faster the longer I carry on suckling on her nipple. She smells of flowers. Of vanilla. Of… Kate.

"The other one," she tells me, breathlessly.

Oh god, yes. Of course. I hold her other breast just firmly enough to guide it in the direction of my face, when she speeds up more, bucking her hips into my thigh. Closer, ever closer… I grab her by the hip and one of her thighs ends up right by my crotch now. Just close enough to…

"Fuck me!" she groans. "If I have to hold out much longer, I'll lose my mind!"

She's on the edge. I can see it in her eyes. And I'm getting hard all over again. Thank god. That's never happened so quickly before either. To disappoint her now would be criminal.

I get up onto my knees beside her. While I'm still fumbling with my button and zip, she's getting out of the rest of her clothes in record time. Her eagerness makes me smile despite my own clumsiness. Still, I finally manage to get my jeans down, along with my damp boxers. I should be embarrassed of that, but there isn't time.

"Do we need, you know…" I mumble, while glancing down at myself.

The way she looked at me. The way she's still looking at me, kneeling on her bed, with my jeans down my thighs, and my hand wrapped around my cock. What does she see that I don't?

"I don't have any condoms," I tell her. It didn't occur to me I'd need any. Hell, I wouldn't even know how to put the bloody thing on in my current state.

She hurriedly shakes her head. "We're good. All I need is you."

Those are the magic words. She spreads and I position myself between her thighs. I know how this works, in theory. And yet… The view of her naked body, presented to me like an unwrapped, much desired gift, is almost too much. I freeze for a second, just trying to catch my breath.

She reaches for my shoulders, guiding me down. My right hand is still down there, trying to help me aim. I can't see what I'm doing. I'm sweating and about to panic all over again, when I feel it. Her warm core, pressed up against the tip of my cock.

Kate grabs my face. Our eyes meet just long enough to steady my spinning thoughts.

"Softly," she whispers. "Slowly!"

I try. God, I try. But now that I know I'm on the right track, I can't help but push down and forward. It's inevitable. It's unstoppable. I never thought it'd be this hot. This tight. It's a good thing I already came once, or else it'd be over before it ever began.

By now, I'm on my elbows, sort of. Mostly I'm on her. In her. Her arms wrap around my neck and her lips press up against mine. I can barely react; I'm too overcome.

But when I start to move… Nothing prepares me for the sensation. I retreat, just a little, just as much as I can bear, before I'm drawn back in. Deep as I can.

"I love you," I hear someone say. Not sure if it's her or me. Maybe it's both of us.

"I love you…"

"Faster," she whines.

I try that too. Mind blowing. Transcendent. She knows best; her wish is my command.

And in between the ragged breaths and whispered encouragement, her lips barely leave mine for a second. Her hands roam freely across my back as well as down, with one of them resting on my ass every so often. I never thought I'd like that. But I do.

I love it. I love everything about this moment. Most of all, her.

How she whimpers and moans. How her hips rise up to meet me, and her legs keep trying to hold onto my waist, but keep flopping down again. How this moment is so messy and sweaty and imperfect. And yet exactly how it's supposed to be.

Although it's awkward, and I'm still not sure of the right rhythm, I keep on going. I keep on trying to make her squeal a little when I go deep and grind into her. She seemed to like it rougher when she was rubbing into my thigh.

She really seems to like this too. Because the words have stopped. Her touch grows erratic, her breaths short. And the pressure seems to build ever more. Until I'm off kilter too, and wavering through the burn that's developing in my thighs.

"Don't…" she pants. "Stop!"

I don't. I won't stop. I'll carry on as long as she needs me to. Till the death.

It doesn't get that far. I keep going, thrusting into

her again and again and again, until she digs her fingernails in hard. Sweet pain. I've earned it.

And then her legs end up around me again, grabbing me, keeping me in place, buried deep inside. Her back arches, eyes open in surprise, as she tries to whisper a scream.

And her body. Her body tenses right to its core. Right onto me; holding me; squeezing me.

As if to say: you're mine. And I'm yours. We are one.

Pleasure washes over me like a wave. Unstoppable like it was the first time. And yet, so much better. So much deeper. It fills me and surrounds me. I can do nothing but stay put and let it explode.

Because we *are* one. A trembling, shuddering mass of sweat and skin and limbs.

Beautifully messy.

Her face is flush; red lips, pink cheeks. With damp hair, sticking to her forehead as well as her temples and even her neck. And she smiles. She smiles and I can't do much more than watch. Because this is my favorite view. This is the mental image I want, every night when I go to sleep and every morning when I wake. Her smile. *Her.*

I roll to the side, taking her with me. She rests her head on my arm and never looks away for a second while we catch our breaths. A comforting silence fills the room. A contentment and calm I've also never felt before. Minutes pass, before I find my words again.

"You are everything," I whisper.

Her eyes widen a little.

"You're a miracle."

"You are," she whispers back. "You're everything I want."

Where have you been all my life?

"Believe me. I'll never leave you," I tell her.

"I'll never leave *you!*" Her words stir something in me. I want to believe her. Desperately.

"Not even if…" my voice trails off.

"If?" Her eyebrows scrunch together in concern. I'm ruining it. I should learn to keep my mouth shut already! "Not even if, what?"

I pause. This might not be the moment. Or it might be the perfect one. Because I need to know. I can't live not knowing. "If, you know… That picture from four years ago… If it all went to hell and—"

"If you gained all the weight back?" she asks. "Of course not! Because you'd still be you! And I love you completely."

I just look at her. The sparkle in her eyes, their color so much darker than normal. They're full of truth. Full of wonder. For a few precious seconds, I let myself drown in them. I let myself believe.

"Would *you?*" she asks. "Would you leave me in that case?"

"No, but that's hardly—"

"I was five months pregnant when *he…*" Kate interjects.

Blake. What an absolute low life. What kind of man leaves a woman while she's carrying his child? His own flesh and blood.

"Never. I would never." I rest my forehead against hers. Not now that I know enough of what she's been through. Enough to keep me from misinterpreting things and getting carried away like I did this week.

Never again. Not a single day will start without me wishing her good morning. Not a single evening will end without me asking about her day. I'll provide for her; protect her; love her in every way I know how. There is no alternative. And maybe one day, I'll get to do all of it in person rather than over the phone. If I'm lucky.

Her lips find mine again, and I can feel them smiling mid-kiss. And I am home. Because as long as we're here, in each other's arms, naked and exposed in body and soul, we can do anything. We can be anything. Together.

"Would you marry me?" I mumble against her lips.

"What?" She pulls away, looking concerned again. "If this is about what Gracie said, I already told her—"

I shake my head. "It's too soon. I know. But, would you? Eventually?"

She pauses, just long enough to make me feel like she's actually considering it.

"Yes. Eventually."

Now we're both smiling again. Because that's all the certainty we needed.

EPILOGUE

* Kate *

December.

We leave for the Christmas party a little late, which is all my fault. And Daniel, being every bit the gentleman he is, waited patiently for nearly three quarters of an hour while I got ready.

It's a good thing Claire sent a car to pick us up, because I probably would have canceled long before then. Not because it's not my kind of scene. Okay, that as well. But it's mostly the timing that bothers me.

As soon as we're alone again, I plan to tell Daniel what's on my mind. I'm giddy. Nervous. Don't know how he will react. God, I hope he'll be happy. Because I am. I mean, I will be if he is. How on earth will I keep myself from blurting it out while we're out? With Claire and the rest of the crew, and a bunch of corporate people from the Home TV network, as well as celebrities, and who knows who else around.

I'm so wrapped up in my own little world of confusion, we barely speak a word on the way to the venue. Maybe we don't need to. Because as long as he's holding my hand, I remain somewhat steady.

"Exciting, huh?" Daniel comments, as we enter the brightly decorated ballroom. It's already bustling with people.

I squeeze his hand for support. He goes one step further and puts his arm around me. Attentive, as always. I love it; *him*. I love him.

I should be enjoying the moment. There will undoubtedly be people here I'll recognize. I do watch a lot of TV. Or at least I used to, before… I might even end up getting introduced to some of them. That prospect has been the only reason I accepted Claire's invitation in the first place. That, and the fact that Daniel seemed kind of excited to meet the crew again. He did get to know them pretty well on set, while trying and failing to film his episode multiple times. Until I came along, that is.

But now… Everything has changed. Everything is about to change even more. My heart is racing and my palms are sweaty. I would have bolted, if not for this amazing man right by my side.

He'd better be happy… If he's not happy, I don't know what the hell I'll do!

"Kate! Daniel!" Claire greets me with a huge grin on her face and gives me a big hug, before shaking Daniel's hand. "Don't you guys look absolutely adorable together!"

"Exactly like you knew we would," I say.

She grins at me. "Don't make me say *I told you so!*"

"Even if it was cheating, just a little bit," Daniel teases. I gently elbow him in the arm.

Claire cocks her head to the side and scrutinizes him with a knowing smile. "I'm sure you forgive me for my little white lie. Sometimes the ends justify the means."

"Well, I for one think it worked out pretty well," I quip.

Daniel turns to me for one of those earth shattering moments of eye contact we like to share. "I wouldn't have things any other way," he says.

"Aww!" Claire says. "I'm so pleased you both came out tonight. With the new project I've been working on, it's been impossible to steal a moment away to catch up. You know how it is."

Same old Claire, always the workaholic. Then again, if I didn't have Gracie, and now Daniel, I might do the same. Keeping busy with an exciting job is miles better than sitting around on the couch, drinking too much wine on your own while binging on Rocky Road ice cream.

"Daniel, don't mind, but I'm going to steal Kate away for a little bit to catch up."

"No worries," Daniel says, smiling briefly at me.

He might not, but I kind of do. Before I'm able to protest, I'm whisked away by Claire. Daniel, meanwhile, attracts the attention of a couple of other somewhat familiar faces in the crowd. Claire's crew members, no doubt.

"So? How's life?" Claire asks.

"It's been amazing. *He's* been amazing, I should say." I smile. "And so good with Gracie as well!"

"And your promotion? They're not working you too hard, I hope?"

I shake my head and let out a short laugh. "Oh, not anymore. I don't know why I didn't put my foot down earlier in hindsight. But it's worked out pretty well."

"What's-her-name had it coming."

"Evelyn. Yeah. And even when I do have to do a little overtime, or attend a meeting, Daniel has been amazingly supportive. Most days, he's the one who picks up Gracie. He even will have started on dinner by the time I get home."

"Wonderful! I knew he'd be a great family man," Claire says. She smiles at me warmly for a few seconds, before seemingly getting distracted. "Oh! Now here's another sight for sore eyes. Don't turn around just yet, okay?"

I freeze, unsure of what exactly I'm supposed to be doing, when we're joined by another couple. The man especially seems super excited to meet Claire and greets her with a warm hug.

"Claire, it's been an age!"

"Ethan! And Sarah. So glad you could both make

it!"

"I wouldn't have missed it for the world. In my line of work, it's rare to be invited to one of these things without having to wear a Press ID around my neck, which immediately seems to scare all the celebs off. All except one, of course," the woman, Sarah, replies.

I finally do turn, smiling politely at the new arrivals. The man is about six foot two and built for comfort, much like Daniel, and the woman, petite and sweet-looking. They steal a quick kiss before turning to look at Claire again.

"So, how's the business been treating you since we parted ways?" Ethan asks.

"Oh, it's been a roller coaster ride, I'll tell you. But the new show did really well for the network, so there might be another season in it for me!"

"Remind me, what was it?" Ethan asks.

"Dating show," his date interjects. "We did a big feature about it before the release of the first episode."

"That's right. Anyway, I want to introduce you guys to one of my oldest friends, Kate, here."

I smile at the two of them and nod. "Nice to meet you. Ethan? And Sarah?"

"Likewise. Are you in showbiz as well?" Ethan asks.

Sarah scrutinizes me for a moment, before her

eyes widen with recognition. "Oh! You were on episode four, weren't you?"

I nod shyly. "Yeah, not entirely voluntarily, but it worked out well enough."

"Oh my god, are you here with Daniel?" Sarah asks. "You remember, Ethan? He was my favorite out of all the candidates!"

Ethan shrugs. "I don't know, I was probably in the kitchen fixing us a snack. That's more my area of expertise."

They share a smile and a loving gaze.

In the kitchen? I frown and shoot Claire a questioning glance. *Wait a minute…*

Claire responds to my non-verbal question with a subtle nod and a smile. The couple turns away for a moment, greeting some other people I don't know.

"He's the guy?" I whisper at her. "The one who took over the canceled cooking show you told me about?"

"He's the guy." She grins. "Absolute genius with chocolate. But you know, shush." She briefly raises her index finger over her lips and winks at me.

How exciting! A rare glimpse behind the curtains of her world. That's probably how they just felt, meeting me. How bizarre. To be here as an outsider as well as a pseudo-celebrity in my own right.

I'm still smiling when I turn and scan the room until I spot Daniel. He looks damn good in that tux he's worn for the occasion. Fits him like a glove.

A girl I recognize from the day we shot our episode waves me over in their direction. "Kate, let's take a picture!" she calls out.

I don't know how I feel about that. But when I see Daniel smiling at me and gesturing at me to stand by his side, I feel my chest swell with pride. That's my man over here. Why *wouldn't* I want to pose for a picture with him? I quickly excuse myself before leaving Claire and joining him again.

"You okay?" he asks under his breath.

"Great, yes," I say.

A few more people I saw on the crew join us and we all pose for a silly selfie.

Just when the picture is taken, and we all relax, we're joined by someone who could not look more out of place if he tried. From the tweed coat to the slacks to the thick-rimmed glasses.

"Whoa, all that's missing to complete that picture is a snifter of brandy and a pipe," I mumble.

Daniel suppresses a chuckle.

"Owen, I'm surprised to see you here!" he says, taking a couple of steps in the man's direction.

They shake hands, in a completely formal, stilted fashion. It's such a contrast to how everyone else greeted Daniel, I'm trying hard not to giggle. So he's the infamous relationship expert from the show. I suppose I've seen him before, but he wasn't really involved with me. Claire and her second-in-command handled all the form filling and everything else.

"Daniel. Looking good."

"Thanks, yes, I've—*we've* been doing well."

Owen smiles so briefly, most people might have missed it. "I can see that. That's great. I'm happy for you both."

"I do have a question for you, if you don't mind," Daniel says.

"Shoot."

"Why me?" Daniel asks.

Owen frowns. "What makes you think I had anything to do with that?"

Daniel makes a face. "The show was your concept. The entire matchmaking process. The way you tried to coach me through it. It follows that you picked the candidates. So, again… Why me?"

Owen looks at him for a few seconds, then makes eye contact with me and smiles. "Because this was my aim all along. To prove that there's a science to attraction and relationships."

"Didn't quite work out the way you planned, though," Daniel remarks.

Owen smiles again. "Not the way I planned, and yet you both were the best proof of concept I could hope for. As I told you before. Your compatibility scores were off the charts. Don't worry, it's all going to be in my book. Keep an eye out for it; it should come out sometime next year."

I can't help but let out a baffled chuckle. Don't tell me. First we were on a reality show, and now this guy is writing a book about the whole thing!

"I expect royalties!" Daniel tells Owen, who laughs and places his hand on Daniel's arm ever so briefly.

"Who needs royalties, when you have true love?" Owen remarks, before turning on his heel and resolutely walking away towards the bar.

"Well that was weird," I comment. Touching, but so very weird.

"That was Owen. He's always been weird," Daniel remarks dryly. "And he totally saved my ass that day."

Our eyes meet and I smile. "I'm glad he did."

"Yeah, me too."

Our little moment of connection is interrupted by the announcement that dinner is about to be served. We're whisked away by Jill, Claire's assistant, who shows us to our table. We're seated with the other contestants, all but one in attendance with their counterpart from the show.

I steal a glance at the adjoining table, where the crew is seated. Claire and Owen sit next to each other, along with Jill, who looks awfully cozy with the big and tall cameraman I tried so hard to ignore on set. They're adorable together.

There's also another girl in her early to mid-twenties, who I remember doing odd jobs like fetching coffee. She's only got eyes for the slightly more mature man to her right, who… OK, this might be the first face I recognize from TV.

"Is that who I think it is?" I ask in a hushed voice. Sean, something, hosts a news satire show I've watched occasionally.

Daniel pauses for a moment and puts his fork down. "Shit, I think it might be. Oh my God, now I understand what Nicole was trying to tell me!"

"Nicole?" I turn to him.

"The make-up artist." He subtly points her out.

"Ah! Yes, *that* Nicole."

"She was saying that Lily was having some issues in her personal life and made some remark that I must not be reading the tabloids."

Shit, I think I read about that. Some scandal involving a girl young enough to be his daughter. Well, that confirms it.

"Isn't he a bit old for her?" I wonder aloud.

Daniel shrugs. "They look happy though, don't they? Love is love."

"Awww! Aren't you the hopeless romantic," I tease, grinning widely when he makes an awkward face.

Our eyes meet. And linger.

And I forget that we were in the middle of dinner with all the other couples from the show. And that there'll be photographers around trying to get as many candid shots as possible of everyone here. I forget about all of it.

Time seems to stand still, while my heart flutters harder than ever before. It tickles. It bubbles up right into my vocal chords. Until I can no longer keep it in.

"Daniel," I say.

He nods briefly and takes my hand underneath the table.

"I have something to tell you."

"So do I," he says.

"I was going to do this at home." I caress his knuckles with my thumb.

"Yeah, me too."

We stare at each other for another endless moment. So much to see. All of it good. All of it perfect.

"I'm—"

Laughter erupts somewhere beside us, at the crew table. But I try not to let it distract me.

"Daniel, I'm—"

Every time I try to say it, my throat closes up. I take a deep breath and focus on the deepness of his eyes. The love I feel when I look at him. And the love he reflects back to me at the same time.

"I'm pregnant."

The ambient noise all around prevents me from hearing it, but I can see him inhale sharply through his mouth. He doesn't let go of my hand. Or look away. He seems frozen in place, mesmerized. As I am every time I really stop and look at him. *God, say something. Are you happy?*

"You are?" he asks, his eyes widening slightly.

I don't know if it's the bright lights overhead, or what, but I'm sweating now. I nod.

"Holy shit." He leans forward, putting his other hand on top of mine. "In that case, it's probably a good thing I went ring shopping earlier this week."

"What?" I breathe.

"I know I already asked once, but that wasn't—It wasn't proper," Daniel says.

"My answer remains the same, though."

"You sure?" he asks.

"Always."

"Shit. I'm going to be a dad," Daniel stammers. "Again."

And then he smiles. And I smile. And nothing else matters but us. The two of us, and Gracie, and her little sibling on the way. It's going to be amazing. It's going to be absolutely perfect. Because he's with me. And I'm with him. Forever.

He wraps his arm around me, and I can't help but lean in.

"I love you," we whisper, with a contented smile and a sigh. Not sure who said it first. Doesn't matter, anyway.

Time seems to stand still. All our surroundings—

the rest of the contestants from the show, the photographers milling around—absolutely everyone seems to fade. All I can do is smile. And try to breathe. And smile some more. Ever since that evening in September when we finally talked things through, when we finally laid ourselves bare in every sense of the word, these have been the happiest three months of my life. *Our life.* Now we are three; sometime next year we'll be four. Five when you count Jack, who has become an integral part of our family as well. And then? I don't know yet. I just know we'll be happy together. Finally after all these years of yearning and hoping, I've got it. The family I always hoped for. With the man of my dreams.

AUTHOR'S NOTE

Thanks so much for reading *Sealed with a Kiss!*

Perhaps you've been following me for a while, perhaps you're new to my work. But now that you're here, I'd like to give you a little background on how this book came to be...

My writing career started all the way back in October 2012 when I took a very deep breath, closed my eyes, crossed my fingers and even my toes and clicked 'Publish' on my first short story. That steamy little piece called *Ladies' Day*, and the book it grew into eventually (Beautiful Stranger) are still relevant today because it features a curvy heroine and her more mature lover. It serves as my first foray into steamy body positive romance.

Since then, I've published a whole bunch of books, in various romance sub genres; as L. Moone I write contemporary, and as Lorelei Moone I write about shifters, vampires and other paranormals. Certain themes tend to repeat themselves throughout my catalogue.

Beauty lies in the eye of the beholder. The hang-ups we tend to have about ourselves and our bodies often aren't shared by the opposite sex. While it's a lot more popular to write about gorgeous curvy ladies and their athletic admirers than the other way around, I've dabbled in both right from the start. I just never felt there was a big market for husky men in romance (my sales numbers supported this notion, unfortunately). 2020 changed that thanks to Jessa Kane and her sexy big boy titles,*Hefty* and *Husky*. My mind was blown, and I absolutely devoured them and couldn't get enough. I'm slowly seeing other authors enter this space, so perhaps the time has come? I hope so, because I'd love to write (and read!) a whole bunch more of these...

The idea for *Sealed with a Kiss* has been with me for a while, even before I started writing the *Husky Men Do It Better* series. It originated over ten years ago, inspired by a British reality dating show called *First Dates*, which had a format close to my fictional show, *Sealed with a Kiss*. Couples go on blind dates at a fancy restaurant, and the audience gets to watch the awkwardness that inevitably unfolds as they first get to know each other. It's all that cringe and awkwardness which fascinates me the most in any romance storyline...

What could be more awkward than two characters who each have their own hang-ups about why they don't deserve love, even though they're desperate for it anyway?

Kate's ex left her while she was still pregnant with Gracie, which convinced her that if even the girl's actual father didn't want to stick around and be with her, why would anyone else want to step in now that she's older? And Daniel is so ashamed of his past issues, he finds it hard to believe that a woman and mother, who seemingly has her life completely figured out, would accept the man he is today, nevermind his past self. Little hints of these insecurities crop up during that awkward first date, but the real mess happens much later, off camera, when both have become more invested in each other...

As it often happens with old ideas, us writers become a little too invested in them and want to do them justice. This happened with *Sealed with a Kiss* as well. I started writing it numerous times, ever since setting up the story in *Best Friends Forever* (the second book in the *Husky Men Do It Better* series), which came out in 2021. If you've been following the series since then, you might have spotted a preorder for this very title pop up not once but twice! Both times I was forced to cancel it, because I wasn't happy with what I had come up with. But now, over two years later, I finally got there. And I think the extra time spent on this story was worth it in the end. I do hope you feel the same. :)

But, enough of all this. If you're like me and you just can't wait to read more Dad Bod titles, you'll be pleased to know that I'm already working on my next book (A curvy girl/big boy crossover story which ties into another series of mine, *Coffee & Curves*), which should hit the shelves sometime in 2024. In the meantime, I would like to point you to some other Big Boy books in my catalogue which are already out: Just Another Day at the Office, All My Heart and One Night Stand.

And that's enough from me. I hope you enjoyed the story as much as I did while writing it, and if you're interested in reading more of my work, perhaps you'll consider signing up for my newsletter. I'll even give you a free short story when you sign up.

x, Lorelei